# LET IT RIDE

Pickup Men, #2

## L.C. CHASE

RIPTIDE PUBLISHING

Riptide Publishing
PO Box 6652
Hillsborough, NJ 08844
www.riptidepublishing.com

Let It Ride (Pickup Men, #2)

Cover Art by L.C. Chase, lcchase.com/design.htm
Editor: Danielle Poiesz
Layout: L.C. Chase, lcchase.com/design.htm

ISBN: 978-1-62649-148-9

First edition
May 2014

Also available in ebook:
ISBN: 978-1-62649-147-2

# LET IT RIDE

Pickup Men, #2

## L.C. CHASE

RIPTIDE
PUBLISHING

*For all those still searching for the other half of their heart.*
*May you find it, embrace it, and cherish it, regardless*
*of the package it comes in.*

*For Danielle, who has the patience of a saint.*
*Thank you.*

*For my dearest friends, who stood by me and*
*helped me through. I love you.*

# TABLE OF CONTENTS

# PROLOGUE

The lips on his were firm, demanding, and sent a blazing fire raging to every corner of his body. Calling it a kiss was too simple for something packed with such intensity, something so far beyond Bridge's imagination but also everything he'd always wanted. He opened his mouth, and the invitation was accepted with impassioned fervor. A tongue pressed in, slid alongside his, wrapped around it, and teased it out. And hell if that didn't turn him on even more. He angled his head to deepen the kiss, to take more, give more, burn more. Noses bumped, a stubbled chin rasped across his, and a deep groan vibrated between them, heating the blood pounding through his veins.

The fire grew, branding his skin from the inside out, burning deeper, and he wanted more. So much more. He pulled the solid body in his arms tighter against his chest until hot, sweaty skin slid against his equally hot, sweaty skin. Dense muscle rolled and flexed under the caress of his hands, hairy legs wrapped around his, pulling him closer until their hard groins met. Every rocking motion and press of flesh had him shaking uncontrollably from the ecstasy of loving and being loved so fully and so freely.

"*Bridge.*"

The familiar voice whispered his name like a prayer. Deep, resonant, and wholly masculine. And like a can of gasoline tossed into the core of a bonfire, it ignited an orgasm that exploded through him, stealing his sight, his hearing, his breath. But what really sent his heart stampeding blindly for escape was the name he shouted in the throes of passion. A name that continued to bounce off the walls of his bedroom.

*Eric.*

Bridge's eyes snapped open, and he stared hard at the ceiling while the faint, bittersweet odor of cum tickled his nostrils and his chest rose and fell in double time. His heart continued to pound as the fading remnants of the best wet dream of his entire life left him feeling more than a little unbalanced. A dream featuring a man—and not just any man, but one man in particular. Eric Palmer, the paramedic he'd met on the rodeo circuit the previous season who'd become fast friends with Bridge and his two best friends since childhood and fellow rodeo men, Marty Fairgrave and Kent Murphy. Eric had been on his mind too often over the past months . . . and as far more than just a friend.

He sucked a ragged gulp of air. "Oh my God. I'm gay."

It wasn't the first time he'd questioned his sexuality, but it had been a long time since he had. He'd fooled around with a guy in college because he was the typical horny kid and sex was sex. Plus, it was all part of the college experience, right? So, why not? He'd also been a little curious about what it would be like and had to admit it had been one of the hottest blowjobs he'd ever received.

But then Silvie DeSantos showed up on campus. He'd fallen madly in lust with her at first sight and decided he must be straight and that had been the end of it.

Until now.

"But . . . I like women," he said aloud, closing his eyes to recall the first day he'd seen Silvie, only to snap them open again when his mental vision filled with Eric's smiling, handsome face. The strong jaw, high cheekbones, and straight nose were wholly masculine, yet striking blue-violet eyes outlined with thick, black lashes and those full, red lips softened his features, making him the most beautiful man Bridge had ever seen. He definitely liked that face—and apparently everything else that went along with it. And he did like women, but then it dawned on him he hadn't really noticed any since he'd met Eric back in the spring when Marty had been injured and Eric had been the on-site paramedic.

Now that he thought about it, he'd always admired an attractive man, too, hadn't he? He'd never been afraid of what anyone would think if he complimented a man. Human bodies were simply beautiful, and he'd always let his appreciation be known. He freely showed affection to the people he cared about, too. Shit, how many times had he kissed Marty and Kent? And in public? Granted, it was only cheek bussing and generally not in big crowds, but still, most men didn't do that to other men. Certainly not the rugged cowboys he worked with on the rodeo circuit.

But Eric . . . that man had tweaked something inside of Bridge from the moment they'd met. Had called up a desire for something he'd thought had been nothing more than a one-time youthful curiosity. And the more time he'd spent around the man, the more he realized how much he enjoyed his company. Looked forward to it.

He turned to stare out the window as the first hint of sunrise bled into what would be a clear day—deep oranges and warm yellows faded into a full spectrum of blues, steadily swallowing the darkness of night.

He inhaled slow and deep, holding his breath for a three beat before exhaling just as slowly, and then he kicked off his bedclothes and looked down at himself. Maybe he wasn't really gay. Maybe he was . . .

"Bisexual, then?" He half expected his dick to stand at attention and answer him. But the member in question lay semi-erect against his thigh, somewhere in that orgasmic afterglow of having just had really great sex . . . Only there hadn't been any *real* sex going on.

Okay, so maybe he needed to run a little test. He plumped the pillow under his shoulders and shifted on the bed, opening his legs wider, and then took another breath to focus himself on his mission.

"Women?" His voice sounded firm and determined, and he stared hard at his crotch while picturing the last woman he'd been with, Diana. She was a barrel racer from Northern Cali. Tall, fit, sharp as a whip, and could bend in more ways than any body should. Bridge Junior gave a halfhearted throb of enthusiasm. Okay, there was interest in the fairer sex.

"Men?" He shifted his mental image to an extremely attractive cowboy he'd once tried to set Marty up with, before Marty spilled the beans about his then deeply closeted boyfriend, champion bull rider Tripp Colby. His cock throbbed again, still not quite ready for action so soon, but definitely just as interested in the rougher sex.

If the idea of being with both a man and a woman appealed, then that made him bisexual, right? But he had one more question to ask. He sighed, preparing himself for an answer he already knew. "Eric Palmer?"

He didn't need to apply any effort to conjure up an image of the sexy paramedic with the sharp New York accent. The man was there in his thoughts 24-7, whether Bridge liked it or not. It had been a few months since the regular season had ended, and with Eric living more than two hours away in Redding, Bridge had only seen him a handful of times for beers and pool with friends. But his face was as clear in Bridge's mind as if he were looking into those unique violet-colored eyes right now.

A slow but determined pulse pushed through the length of his cock, and another chased it. Then another, and the pace quickened.

*Yep. Definitely perking up now.*

He glared at his dick and fisted his hands in the sheets to keep from touching himself. "You realize you're getting hard for a man, right?"

Junior responded to his accusation with another eager pump of blood, growing more insistent with each pulse. Greedy bastard.

Bridge barked out a laugh, and a surprising wave of relief washed through him, as if a weight he hadn't known he'd been carrying had lifted. "Well, hell."

Yes, he'd questioned it when he was younger. Yes, he'd once fooled around with a man and enjoyed it. But then a woman had captured his interest, so he hadn't given the whole sexuality thing much more thought after that.

And then along came Eric Palmer, bringing all those questions back to the surface. Only this time, he'd found his answer, and it came without any doubt. Maybe he was gay, maybe he was bisexual, but neither label mattered. Labels were too damn limiting to be set in stone anyway. It was what it was. Like the steady tick of the grandfather clock at the end of the hall and the gentle stirrings of the waking ranch outside his window as the sun's rays crept over the ledge and spilled onto the floor. Life had its own plan; folks just had to learn how to ride it or get bucked off.

Man or woman didn't matter. Marty liked men, Kent liked women, and Bridge apparently liked both.

But Eric was the one he wanted above all others, and for whatever reason, that felt all kinds of right.

He let his head sink back into the pillow and closed his eyes, giving his imagination free rein to run with Eric on its back. He took himself in hand and stroked slowly, picturing Eric tugging on him, Eric's mouth with those plump, red lips sucking on his balls, Eric looking up at him with desire in those amazing eyes. And that was all it took. A few more quick, hard pulls, and his second orgasm of the morning rolled through him.

He threw an arm over his face, absently wiping cum off his action hand onto his stomach, and started laughing.

"Shit. I'm Eric-sexual."

# CHAPTER ONE

*Two months later . . .*

B ridge leaned forward in his seat and gripped the wheel a little tighter. Not to keep the equine RV under control as he steered onto the rodeo grounds at Folsom, but to keep from jumping clean out of his hide. Blood pounded through his veins so fast his skin tingled and his brains felt loose and floaty inside his skull. Then there was the herd of wild horses charging through his stomach, leaving a jittery mess of exposed nerves in their wake. Anticipation overload. Thank God he hadn't drunk any coffee this morning or he'd probably be having a coronary right about now.

"Wanna share?"

Kent's voice jolted Bridge out of his thoughts, but he hoped the truck bouncing through a pothole just then masked his surprise. The big Dodge lurched again when the trailer hit the same hole, and a loud *thud* let him know the horses weren't too happy about it either. He shot a quick glance at Kent, who sat in the passenger seat watching him, eyes hidden behind dark sunglasses, cowboy hat low on his brow, but there was an amused lift to his mouth.

Bridge returned his focus to the driveway. Folsom's rodeo grounds were part of a park that sat along the banks of the American River. A densely tree-lined road led the way to the main spectator parking area and then wrapped around behind the arena to the designated lot for competitors and crew, which was half-hidden by more trees. The first lot was empty, as he'd expected, but he didn't have a clear view of the one behind yet. Damn trees were going to make him wait until the last minute to see if Eric's truck was already there.

He managed to keep his voice casual. "Share what?"

"Why you're smiling," Kent said. "I know you didn't get laid last night, so what is it?"

*Damn*. Bridge hadn't realized he'd been smiling like a crushing high schooler.

He cast another sideways look at Kent and shifted in his seat. *Well. It's like this, Kent. I get to see Eric again today—for four whole days, actually—and I'm really excited because I've been having erotic dreams about him for months now, and maybe if I'm lucky, it wasn't all fantasy and I really will get laid this weekend.*

But he couldn't spill that out of the blue without some sort of preamble, could he?

"I'm just looking forward to getting back at it," he said instead, steering his rig around the far side of the arena.

"I am too, but this is only a preseason clinic. Nothing to get *that* excited about." Kent's tone said he didn't buy Bridge's answer for a second. Bridge had known he wouldn't. The annual rodeo school was a great way to teach greenhorns a few things and introduce new cowboys to the sport. Kent taught roping sessions, and Bridge and Marty worked pickup, as well as ran a session on their profession. And while it was fun, it wasn't *that* exciting. Not unless he was the greenhorn. "And this is far from your first rodeo, cowboy."

"I know. I'm just excited to see the guys again. Marty and Tripp." Bridge rolled his hands on the wheel. "And Eric. It's been too long."

"Yeah, it has." Kent finally turned his attention to the grounds in front of them, and Bridge felt Kent's all-too-observant stare fall off him as if it had been a brick sitting on his chest. But the feeling was fleeting. The sense of lightness that had him on the cusp of floating out of his seat the whole drive left him when he pulled into the parking area and found it empty. His body sank back into the seat like a deflating balloon.

"Told you we'd be the first ones here," Kent said. "I don't know why you were in such a rush to get going, especially since this is pretty much our backyard."

Bridge ignored his best friend and guided the rig toward the back of the grass lot and parked. Kent hopped out of the cab, and Bridge hung back for a second to release a long breath before following. "Chill, dude," he mumbled to himself. "It's just Eric."

He huffed a short laugh and shook his head. There was nothing *just* about Eric Palmer. He took another deep breath and ran his hands over his thighs, then exited the truck and met Kent at the back of the rig. Together, they went about their practiced routine of unloading the horses and tethering them to hooks welded along the outside of the trailer. Once the horses were secure, Kent climbed up the short ladder on the side of the big fifth wheel.

"You're going to tell me what's had you practically whistling like a kid on his way to Disneyland the last few days." Kent's disembodied voice carried down from the roof of the rig, followed by a grunt. The trailer rocked, and Bridge jumped back when a bale of alfalfa came flying at him without warning, landing where he'd just been standing.

Kent peered over the edge, a cocky grin on his face. Bridge glared up at him. "Dude. That was a bit close."

Kent snorted and put his hands on his hips. "Met a new girl, right?"

"What? No." He shook his head. "There's no girl." He pulled a Swiss Army knife from his belt loop and leaned down to slice the baling twine. "I told you. Just excited to get on with rodeo season."

"Which doesn't officially start for another two weeks."

True, but he wasn't ready to share what had him feeling like a five-year-old on Christmas Eve yet. He had to see Eric first. Make sure he wasn't building up some wild imaginary love affair that would never exist beyond a few crazy dreams. Okay, there'd been a lot more than *a few* dreams, and the only crazy thing about them was how much he wanted them to come true, but still . . .

"Shut up and throw down another bale."

Kent disappeared from view, but his laugh echoed across the empty lot. Bridge began splitting leaves off the bale and putting them in the mesh feed bags they'd strung up between their five horses. Kent, a state champion steer wrestler, only needed one horse, but as a pickup man, Bridge worked all day every day and needed fresh horses with different abilities for specific events. Light, fast, and agile for the bronco and roping events, and a big, solid horse that could handle tangling with a two-thousand-pound beast, if it came to it, for the bull-riding events. In general, though, that was a scenario they all made a point of avoiding. His job was to make sure every cowboy and animal that entered the ring left it safely. Including himself.

The low rumble of a heavy-duty engine drew his attention just as Kent climbed down from the roof of the trailer.

"Here they are," Kent said. Excitement laced his smooth voice, and Bridge had to laugh. He smacked the brim of Kent's hat, knocking it askew.

"Who's the excited one now?"

"Hey!" Kent adjusted his hat, shaking his head, and stepped over to stand beside him, bumping shoulders with him. Bridge smiled and threw an arm over his shoulder. Kent was a few inches shorter than him—about the same height as Eric—and he wondered if Eric would tuck under his arm as comfortably as Kent did.

They both waved as Marty approached in his own equine RV—not quite as big as Bridge's because he only had four horses to haul, but still impressive. Marty angled his rig parallel to Bridge's, cab to trailer so their doors opened to each other, as they always did, in their own circling-the-wagons kind of way. The tradition stemmed from when they'd first started working as pickup men, and some of the good old boys hadn't been too keen on Marty's out-and-proud presence, so they'd parked their rigs this way to create a safety barrier of sorts. After a few years, the regulars began to accept that Marty's orientation had zero bearing on how well he did his job, and things, while not completely safe, were safer, but their parking habit remained the same.

Marty jumped down from the cab of his truck, a huge smile splitting his handsome face, and threw himself at Bridge. They were the same height, though Bridge packed more muscle and bulk, but that didn't stop the air from whooshing from his lungs on impact. He stumbled back into one of his horses, who gave a disinterested swish of his tail and continued munching his hay. Bridge wrapped his arms around Marty and hugged him tightly.

"Man, you're a sight for sore eyes," Bridge said, his voice tight with emotion. They'd only seen Marty a few times since Marty and Tripp had gotten back together after a nasty breakup at the end of last season. It had been a tough time, but the two of them were working through and finding their happiness. And seeing Marty's light shine so bright always had a way of reminding Bridge that all was right with the world.

Marty stepped back, holding Bridge's arms by the biceps. His green eyes glittered with joy. "You're looking good, B."

He gave a squeeze, and then he let go, turning to wrap Kent up in another bone crusher of a hug.

"I miss seeing you guys all the time," Marty said when he let Kent go.

"Same here, Smarts," Bridge said, and Kent nodded.

Tripp hobbled up beside Marty. He'd never walk without a cane again, but he was moving with much more confidence now than the last time Bridge had seen them. Marty slid his arm around Tripp's waist, and a light blush crested over Tripp's cheeks, his mouth lifting in a shy, crooked smile. That was something Bridge never thought he'd see—Tripp accepting any kind of PDA, let alone acknowledgment of Marty in public—but he was damn glad for his best friend that Tripp had finally broken out of the closet. Bridge approved of this new more relaxed and expressive Tripp.

"Hey, Bridge." Tripp held out his hand. "Good to see you again."

"Screw that." He knocked Tripp's hand away and pulled him into a solid hug. They'd had their differences, but Tripp had earned his respect when he came out and made a stand for Marty. Even though it had cost him his career. "You're family now, dude. How many times do I have to tell you that?"

Tripp laughed and stepped back, holding a hand up in surrender. "Okay, okay. I got it." Then he turned and accepted a hug and playful smack on the back from Kent. Bridge caught Marty looking at him, his gaze warm and shiny, like tears might be brewing. *Thank you*, he mouthed. Bridge smiled back and nodded.

With greetings out of the way, they went back to setting up for the weekend, but he couldn't really concentrate. Every ten minutes, he looked at his wristwatch. Every distant rumble of a vehicle engine had him inconspicuously peeking around the trailers.

The afternoon progressed slowly, and the sun began its determined descent toward the horizon, pushing long shadows out across the spring grass. The constant rise and drop of adrenaline in his system was beginning to wear on him. Maybe he'd saddle up Breeze and go for a ride along the river trail. Kill some time and try to settle his nerves. He lifted his hat and ran a hand through his hair, then turned around, and his heart shot into his throat, choking off the ability to breathe, speak, or even think.

Eric, the man of his dreams—literally—stood near the back of Marty's rig looking way too sexy in worn jeans, sneakers, and a turquoise golf shirt fitting tight enough to show off the hard muscle beneath. His short-cropped, dark-blond hair sparkled like gold in the sun's fading rays. A single dimple bracketed one side of a warm and friendly smile.

"Hey, guys." Eric addressed them as a group, but his sharply accented voice coasted over Bridge like an intimate caress, sending a rush of heat southward to pool in his groin.

He hung back, rendered immobile by Eric, live and large just ten feet away from him, and watched while his friends greeted his walking wet dream one by one with hugs, backslaps, and smiles. He'd worried that he'd spent too long in his fantasies, that his imagination had blown everything out of proportion and he wasn't really physically attracted to Eric, but the second the paramedic walked in his direction and engulfed him in a hearty hug, every doubt he'd ever entertained vanished. Feeling Eric's body so close, the heat that radiated from him and bled into Bridge, and smelling the tantalizing spice-and-citrus scent of Eric's cologne, proved his dreams were far from exaggerated. They had been nothing but a poor tease of the real thing.

He fought the urge to bury his nose in Eric's neck, to suck an earlobe into his mouth, and to keep his body from showing just how happy he was to see Eric again, but he couldn't let go of his living fantasy either. Eric broke the embrace first and looked up at him with those captivating eyes, so much more intense in person. "Good to see you again, Bridge."

"Yeah." He cleared his throat, but his voice sounded a bit too deep and husky to his ears. "You too." *You don't even know.*

Oblivious to the raging hormones wreaking havoc on Bridge's libido, Eric turned and clapped his hands twice. "Well, what the hell are you all standing around for? Let's go get some grub and play some pool!"

"Thanks, sweetheart," Bridge said, taking the fresh pitcher of beer from the waitress and then dropping a couple of bills on her empty tray in its place. She looked up at him through long eyelashes and smiled.

"Can I get you anything else?" Her voice practically purred, and the slight raise of one dark eyebrow clued him in to the fact she was offering more than a fresh bowl of peanuts or another round of chicken wings. She was definitely pretty—long, dark hair fell loose over her bare shoulders, a short skirt showed off long legs, and a tank top displayed the rest of her God-given assets—and though he would have definitely been interested not all that long ago, he now had his sights too firmly set on someone else.

He shook his head and smiled. "We're all set."

"Okay. Well . . ." Her pout was subtle, but she stepped closer and pressed a napkin into his hand. "If you change your mind."

*Don't hold your breath, darlin'.* He tipped his hat, and she turned, casting a seductive look over her shoulder before walking away with a little extra swing of her hips.

Kent stepped up beside him and began to refill his beer mug. "She's sexy. Get her number?"

Bridge shrugged and dropped the napkin—he knew without looking that it had her digits on it—on the table in front of Kent. "Here. Give her a call."

Kent stopped mid-pour and nearly dropped the pitcher back on the table. His eyebrows disappeared under the brim of his hat, and his mouth fell open. "Since when do you turn away a hot girl like that?"

"What's going on?" Eric said, coming up behind Bridge and reaching for the pitcher to top off his beer, saving him from having to come up with a quick answer. "You look a little shocked there, Kent." He stood close enough for Bridge to catch another whiff of his cologne. Damn, but the man smelled good. Bridge couldn't stop himself from shifting a little closer and inhaling a little deeper.

"Nothing," Bridge said. He didn't know how to tell his friends what was going on yet, and he had to find out if Eric could be on the same page first. What was the point of telling them he might be gay, or bi most likely, if the only man he was interested in wasn't interested in him?

Kent snorted. "B has a new girl he's not telling us about."

Eric frowned. "You do?" He stepped closer to the table, probably to hear Kent better over the almost-too-loud music in the sports bar they'd wandered into. His arm brushed Bridge's when he lifted his mug to take a sip. The touch was light, unintentional, but the effect was still enough to send a thrill coursing through Bridge's veins. He took a swig of his beer and swallowed hard.

"Who's got a girl?" Marty said, holding the pool cue out toward Kent. "Your turn."

"B's been singing and smiling to himself for a few days now," Kent said. He took a quick drink before taking the cue stick from Marty. "And I swear he drank an entire pot of coffee this morning, with the way he was pinging around the truck on the drive here today."

"I was not pinging." Bridge straightened to his full height and puffed his chest out a little. "And I already told you, there's no girl."

Kent gave him a skeptical look and then shook his head before walking over to the pool table to take his shot. Bridge looked back at Marty and Eric, both watching him with curious expressions.

"There's not!"

Marty and Eric shared a glance but didn't saying anything. They didn't need to. Bridge could read the disbelief in their amused smiles. He rolled his eyes and took a long draught of his beer.

Tripp returned from the bar with a bag of ice for his leg and reclaimed his stool beside Marty. They'd been taking turns playing doubles pool since they were odd numbered, but Tripp's leg had begun to hurt so he'd decided to take up a referee position from their table while Marty and Eric teamed up against Bridge and Kent. Tripp looked from one to the other and then settled on Marty. "What did I miss?"

"B!" Kent called from the other side of the table. "You're up."

*Saved!* He set down his drink and turned so quickly he jostled Eric, who'd just raised his mug to his mouth. Beer spilled over the lip of the tipped glass and dribbled down Eric's chin. Bridge reached out to steady himself by placing one hand on the table and the other on Eric's hip but froze when the amber liquid dripping onto Eric's chest caught his attention. All he wanted to do right then was lean down and slide his tongue over that wet, exposed skin. He licked his lips and lifted his gaze to meet Eric's. He couldn't get a read on Eric's expression, but he was sure he saw a flash of heat in the violet depths of his eyes; that in their fleeting look, Eric somehow knew what was going on in Bridge's head, knew what kinds of dreams he'd been having, and just maybe felt a little of the same.

Kent called to him again, an impatient note in his voice, and the brief connection broke.

"Shit. I'm sorry, dude." Bridge grabbed a napkin, the one with the waitress's phone number on it, and handed it to Eric. He turned away before he could use the napkin as an excuse to touch Eric and dab away the alcohol himself, run his hands over places *just friends* had no business running their hands.

Kent passed off the cue with a raised eyebrow, but Bridge ignored him. He focused on the task of chalking the cue stick to get back to center. When he felt somewhat collected again, he cleared his throat. "Five ball, corner pocket," he called to no one in particular and then leaned down. He spread his legs a little, pulled the stick back, and then he glanced up at the mirrored wall on the other side of the table and froze. He'd called a shot that had him bent over the table right in front of Eric, and in the reflection, he could see that Eric had noticed. His gaze was planted firmly on Bridge's ass.

Encouraged, Bridge didn't move, waiting until their eyes met in the glass. When they did, he gave his butt a little wiggle. "Checking out my ass, Palmer?" he teased over his shoulder.

Eric snorted, leaning back on his stool a little. "In your dreams, Sullivan."

*Oh, you don't know the half of it.* Bridge winked and then turned his attention back to the pool table. A smile spread across his face of its own volition, and he rocked from foot to foot until Kent yelled at him to hit a damn ball already. He settled into position, lined up, and snapped the shot. The cue ball bounced off the three ball, which careened into the five ball and sent it cleanly into the corner pocket. He pumped his fist in the air and hooted. Marty's and Kent's groans were offset by a whistle and enthusiastic applause from Eric. Bridge tipped his hat at Eric, then called out his next shot. This time he had to set up on the opposite side of the table, but when he had his strategy planned out, he raised his eyes to meet Eric's and grinned. When Eric shifted in his seat, Bridge took the shot. And missed.

"Your turn," Bridge said, inducing a hint of challenge in his voice.

Eric jumped down from his barstool and met Bridge in front of the pool table. Bridge held the cue stick out for him but didn't let go when Eric grabbed it. Their gazes locked for an extended beat, and then Eric stepped into Bridge's space. That spicy-citrus fragrance drifted into his nostrils, teasing his senses and triggering a rush of endorphins in his brain.

"If I didn't know any better—" Eric's voice was low, his accent thicker. His hand slid down the shaft of the stick until it rested above Bridge's, and the contact sent a burning spike of arousal careening into Bridge's cock. "—I'd think you were flirting with me."

"Maybe you don't know better," Bridge said, quietly enough for only Eric to hear, and then grinned when his eyes widened ever so slightly. Bridge let go of the cue stick, dropping his hand to brush Eric's thigh as he walked past him without looking back.

He made it to their table without tripping over his boots and took a long draught of his beer. His heart pounded in his chest as if he'd just run five miles, his mouth had gone dry, and his jeans were feeling damned uncomfortable. He'd basically just tipped his hand. Risky, he knew. He did not want to screw up a great friendship, but at the same time, he had to know if it could be more.

Fortunately, Marty and Tripp were otherwise engaged in their own private conversation and not paying attention to Bridge or the game, but Kent's keen gaze didn't miss much. Bridge knew full well that the slight frown on his friend's face meant *We'll be talking later.*

Eric called his shot, and Bridge turned around, grateful to get out from under Kent's stare. He wasn't ready to tell Kent that the girl he thought had Bridge skipping was actually Eric. Of all the people he knew, his best friends would be the most understanding. They'd even jokingly asked if he had something to tell them a time or two in the past. But until he knew where things stood with Eric, he couldn't share with them just yet.

Eric looked up at him then, and once again, Bridge's heart shot into his throat while blood flooded into his groin fast enough to make his head spin.

*Shit, I really am in for it.*

# CHAPTER
## TWO

E ric watched the action in full swing at the center of the arena with rapt attention. His gaze wasn't on the man riding the bronco, who was losing control and coming dangerously close to meeting the ground with his face rather than his feet, but on the pickup men flanking the bucking horse, trying to pull its rider to safety. And he was focused on one pickup man in particular: Bridge Sullivan. The cowboy who'd look just at home on a surfboard as he did on a horse. His too-long blond hair had kept Eric awake all night, imagining what it would feel like sliding through his fingers. And then there were the Superman jawline and cleft chin, and those deep-brown, gold-flecked eyes that had stared down at him with so much heat and intensity last night in the bar that he'd almost imploded on the spot.

He shifted, reliving that look as if it were happening right now, and propped a foot on the railing to mask the need to adjust himself. Then he scolded himself for thinking things he shouldn't be thinking about a friend and a colleague. He was here to do a job, not fantasize.

Focus renewed, he watched Bridge lean down and yank a flapping tail of rope to release the horse's flank strap while the cowboy half jumped, half slid from the bronco to Marty's horse, then to the ground. There was no grace in the cowboy's dismount, but this weekend's competitors were students learning the necessary skills to reach the pro-tour level. A little shaky looking but otherwise okay, the cowboy made his way out of the arena while Bridge guided the bronco toward the exit gate. The bronc snorted and threw its head, spinning around in an attempted escape, but Bridge anticipated the move, and with subtle commands, his horse about-faced and bolted ahead of the runaway steed. The smooth, relaxed way Bridge sat in his saddle, the thick muscular thighs that seemed glued to his horse's side, and how his shirt stretched across his broad back as he reined his horse with one hand and swung the lasso with the other captivated Eric.

With the bronco and cowboy safely out of the ring and the crew preparing for the next ride, Bridge and Marty rode back to their guard point beside the chutes. Bridge scanned the rails, and his gaze landed on Eric by the arena exit, where he was stationed for quick access in case of emergency. Even from across the arena and shadowed under the brim of his hat, that stare punched Eric dead center in his solar plexus. Bridge tipped his hat once before returning his attention to his job.

*Jesus.* Eric ran a finger along the collar of his shirt, pulling it away from his skin to catch a bit of breeze. Why was a man he'd been told was straight pinging his gaydar so hard? Especially at times like now, when Bridge kept looking over at him. Stealing quick glances as though he was making sure Eric was still there or to see if Eric was watching him.

Then there was the way Bridge had flirted with him last night . . . At first he'd thought Bridge had just had a few too many drinks and had been trying to get a rise out of him, but the burning fire in those warm eyes . . . That wasn't a man playing—that man had wanted him. Eric knew it right down to his very marrow. Bridge was not at all as straight as everyone seemed to think.

And therein lay the problem.

Last year, when he'd just met them all, if Bridge had pulled what he had last night, Eric would've taken him home in a heartbeat. But things had changed. Now Bridge, Marty, and Kent had become the best and closest friends he'd had in as long as he could remember. A situation that made him want to bounce with happiness, and at the same time retreat behind the self-made shield that protected him from ever being let down again. At some point, the party would end like it always did—or be taken away from him—so that layer of protection was necessary. But for the first time in years, he'd allowed himself to make friends. More than that, for as relatively new as his friendship with them was, he felt as if he'd always known the trio, and that sense of complete acceptance kept him hanging around and settling deeper into their fold.

He would not make a mess of things by letting himself fall for Bridge—who may or may not even play for his team. If he did that and things went the way they always did, he'd end up losing them all. And that was a risk he wasn't willing to take.

"Here, man." Eric jumped at the sound of Tripp's voice right next to him, so lost in his thoughts that he hadn't heard the man approach. "Coffee."

Grateful for the yank back to reality, he took the paper tray that held two cups of steaming black liquid from Tripp, who'd carried it from the concession stand balanced carefully in his right hand. His left was on the cane he'd need for the rest of his life after the damage his leg had suffered from a brutal beating when he'd publicly come out at the end of last season. But the man was damned determined to fend for himself and not let anyone coddle him in any way; he'd insisted on getting coffee for the two of them on his own. Eric pulled one cup from the tray and handed it to Tripp, then lifted the other out for himself and tossed the tray into a large blue barrel near the arena exit.

He lifted his cup in Tripp's direction before taking a sip. "Thank you."

Tripp nodded. "How're things looking out there? Any of those rookies busting their skulls open yet?"

"Let's hope not," Eric said, sending up a silent prayer. He was trained to deal with most every emergency, but he enjoyed his job the most when it was boring. He preferred people staying healthy and whole. "It's nice and quiet, just the way I like it."

"Yeah, but where's the fun in that?" Tripp said, amusement clear in his voice and a mischievous glint in his cool-blue eyes. "It's all about the mayhem."

Eric shook his head. "So the stories are true. You bull riders really are nuts."

Tripp laughed, turning his attention to the ring, and the expression on his rugged face softened. Bridge and Marty rode side by side toward them, and Marty graced Tripp with a smile that could make even the coldest heart melt. Eric knew Tripp's had a long time ago. The ex-bull rider's smile widened, his fear of anyone knowing the two even knew each other, let alone were together, fading more and more with each passing day. It warmed Eric to see that growing confidence. No one should ever have to live in fear of showing another how much he means to him.

"How's it going out there?" Tripp reached through the metal rails to stroke the thick neck of Marty's horse.

Marty glanced over his shoulder. "Not bad. Couple of cowboys are going to find themselves in a world of hurt if they don't pay attention, though."

"Bunch of greenhorns." Bridge laughed, and the deep rumble of his voice drew Eric's gaze to the big cowboy astride the equally big chestnut gelding. Their eyes met, locked, and there it was again, that flare of heat he'd seen the night before in those melted-chocolate eyes. The kind of look that clearly said *I want you* and set off Eric's bells and whistles like a pinball machine.

Time stilled. Voices and pounding hooves and lowing livestock faded. A light breeze gently lifted the ends of Bridge's hair, like gold threads of silk, and the tips of Eric's fingers tingled, wanting to touch.

"C'mon, B. Gotta get back to it." Marty broke the frozen moment, and Eric remembered to breathe.

Bridge nodded ever so slightly, eyes still on Eric, and then reined his horse after Marty and headed back into the action. Eric put a hand on the railing, needing something solid to hold on to for a minute while he watched Bridge ride away, watched the way his broad shoulders rocked with the sway of his horse, the way the muscles in his arms bulged when he adjusted the spoke of his lasso, the way he turned his head and scanned the arena, completely aware of every animal and cowboy in the ring. Confident, sexy, loyal, and everything Eric had ever imagined a cowboy would be.

Everything he wanted in a man.

Shit. His maybe-not-so-straight friend was going to make it hard to keep his boundaries in place.

The five of them sat at a picnic table during intermission, eating burgers and drinking cold colas while sharing the morning's highlights from the first of four days at rodeo school. Bridge and Kent sat on one side, Marty between Tripp and Eric on the other.

Bridge's gaze kept wandering from Marty and Tripp to Eric, and he found his attention more on Eric and less on the conversation.

Marty leaned in and whispered something in Tripp's ear. Tripp looked down so the brim of his hat covered most of his face, but not enough to hide the smile that Bridge saw lift his mouth. Marty sat back up and popped a French fry into his mouth, looking rather proud of himself as he chewed. He caught Bridge's eye and winked, which made Bridge smile too. This was the Marty he'd missed so much. It had been a hard road for those two, and at one time, he'd hated Tripp for the way he'd treated Marty. But now that he understood Tripp's reasons, and what he'd had to overcome in order to be the man Marty deserved, Bridge had come to realize Tripp really was the perfect man for his best friend. And there was no denying they were clearly head over boots in love with one another.

Bridge slid his gaze back to Eric, and his breath caught. Eric was watching him, his expression unreadable, but a little thrill still charged through his veins.

"Right, Bridge?"

He jerked at the sound of his name. "Huh?"

"Dude." Marty sighed, lowering the French fry that had only made it halfway to his mouth. "What's with you?"

"What? Nothing." Bridge shifted on the hard wood bench, trying to remember where he'd dropped the thread of their conversion while ignoring the glance Marty and Kent exchanged. He also made a point of not looking at Eric. Nope. Definitely *not* looking at Eric.

"Lady Loooove," Kent singsonged under his breath before taking a big bite of his burger.

"Oh my God. Will you stop?" Bridge growled, his gaze shooting in Eric's direction. "There is no girl."

Kent chuckled around the food in his mouth, and Bridge elbowed him playfully while Marty continued to stare at him. He could see the wheels turning in his friend's head and the moment he let it go. Thankfully. Bridge knew it was only a temporary reprieve, but he'd take what he could get for now.

"I was saying," Marty intoned while giving him the *pay attention* glare. "I think that young cowboy, Cory Ackerson, will make a great pickup man. He seemed to know every move the animals were going to make before they made them. That's a talent you're born with."

"Yep," Bridge agreed, grateful the conversation had picked up where it had apparently left off. He reached for his drink. "He'll be an asset to the circuit."

"Not our circuit, though," Marty said.

"No?"

Marty shook his head and turned to Tripp. "You should have a talk with him. He wants to ride pickup for the IGRA."

"What's the IGRA?" Eric asked.

"International Gay Rodeo Association," Tripp said. "I've contacted them about teaching bull riding and using what pull my name still has to help bring more awareness and acceptance for other gay cowboys stuck in the closet."

"Cool." Eric leaned forward to look fully at Tripp. "So, can you teach me to ride?"

Bridge choked on the soda he'd just swallowed, bubbles burning his nostrils. "No!" The word was out before he'd even realized the thought had crossed his mind, and four sets of surprised eyes landed on him. Heat rose in his cheeks. "I mean, bull riding is for psychos." *Shit.* "No offense, Tripp."

Tripp chuckled, and a crooked smile spread across his face. "None taken. Goes with the territory."

Bridge put down his drink and looked at Eric. He tried to play it cool, but his words spilled out in a rush. "Just, you know, it's one of the most dangerous sports going, and I've seen too many guys' careers—and a few lives—come to end from riding those crazy-ass animals. Not to mention, we've never seen you ride a horse, so you shouldn't be even thinking about getting up on a bull."

*Not ever, if I have my way.*

Silence fell over the table while the sounds of rodeo life around them amplified in Bridge's eardrums. Horses and cattle stamping their hooves, whinnying and lowing—it sounded like there was a whole herd right behind him. Voices rose over the livestock in a steady but indistinguishable din, broken at random intervals by hearty laughter, and the unmistakable sizzling of burger patties and hot dogs on the open grill played in the background. All the while, his heart raced and heat flushed over the surface of his skin; perspiration broke out across the back of his neck, and for the life of him, he couldn't figure out what to say next.

A grin unfolded on Eric's face, capped by a single dimple. He placed a hand over his chest. "Aww . . ." His voice was light, teasing, and he fluttered his long eyelashes. "I didn't know you cared."

The rest of the guys started laughing, and Bridge relaxed a little, joining in at his own expense. He chucked a French fry across the table, and it bounced off Eric's chin, landing squarely on his paper plate. "You're just too irresistible."

Eric preened. "Knew it." Then he picked up the fry and popped it into his mouth, chewing with exaggerated flourish. Bridge shook his head.

"Yeah," Tripp finally said, getting the convo back on point and backing Bridge up, whether he realized it or not. "Bull riding isn't for everyone, and it's not a matter of *if* you'll break something, but *when*." He turned toward Eric. "We need guys like you on the ground to patch us up so psychos like me can get back in the saddle."

"Good point," Eric conceded. "I've actually never broken a bone."

"Knock on wood, buddy," Kent mumbled.

Tripp laughed. "And I don't think I have a single one that hasn't been broke."

"And on that note . . ." Marty stood up and nudged Tripp's shoulder, thankfully ending the current discussion. "We have a couple of things to . . . take care of before the afternoon sessions start."

Bridge didn't have to use too much imagination to guess what those "couple of things" were. His mind had been running scenarios of him with a certain paramedic too often to stretch it very far. "Just remember to put your shirt back on right side out."

"Who says we'll bother wasting time by taking shirts off?" Marty rebounded with a serious note in his voice, but the smirk on his face elicited laughter from the table.

Bridge watched them walk away and smiled when he saw Marty reach out and let his fingers brush the back of Tripp's hand. Tripp hooked his pinky around Marty's. The move was hesitant, covert, but profound nonetheless. When Bridge turned back to the table, he found Eric watching him with those striking eyes. Heat crept into his cheeks again, and he looked down at his plate for a distraction, only to find it empty.

Eric cleared his throat. "Yeah, I should go get my kit ready." He rose from the table and began gathering the discards of their lunch. "You guys all done?"

Bridge and Kent nodded in unison. "Thanks, dude."

"See ya later?" Bridge meant it to be a casual *later* but somehow it became a question. Almost eager.

Eric lifted a brow a notch and then tipped his head. "Yeah. See ya later." His gaze shot quickly to Kent and then he turned with hands full, heading for the nearby garbage barrel.

Bridge couldn't help but watch Eric walk away, eyes locked on the way his dark-blue work trousers hugged his firm, round ass.

"So . . ." Kent began when Eric was out of earshot, throwing their plates, cups, and wrappers in the trash. "Going to tell me what's going on now?"

"Nope." Bridge tore his gaze from ogling Eric, hoping Kent hadn't realized that's what he'd been doing, and casually scanned the empty arena.

"There's really no new girl?"

Bridge slanted a sideways glance at him. "Like I said."

Kent remained silent for so long that Bridge sighed and turned to look at him fully, only to feel like a bug under a microscope with the way Kent stared at him. He knew Kent was reading him like an open book, because really, he was one. He knew that. He didn't hold much back, didn't worry what anyone thought about much of anything. He just wanted to rodeo and enjoy life and make his friends laugh. But that didn't stop him from shifting on the bench again. When the hell did the thing get so damned uncomfortable?

"What?"

Kent shrugged. "You know you can tell me anything, right?" Nothing in his voice or eyes but concern. "And Marty."

Bridge didn't miss the emphasis Kent put on those last two words. He just nodded. "Yeah."

Kent clapped him on the shoulder and stood. "I love you, man."

Bridge looked up into friendly blue eyes and smiled at Kent's unwavering acceptance and loyalty. "Love you back."

Bridge held out his fist, and Kent bumped it with his knuckles. Then he smiled that suave James Bond smile of his that always won the ladies over. "I got some rookies to go show how to wrestle down a seven-hundred-pound steer now."

Bridge nodded. "See you out there."

He watched Kent walk away and exhaled a long breath, then lifted his hat and ran a hand through his hair. He really needed to get Eric alone and have a talk. Soon.

# CHAPTER
## THREE

"You all right?" Eric asked when Kent brought his horse to a halt beside him, wincing as he dismounted.

There were still a couple more sessions on the roster, but day one of rodeo school was coming to an injury-free close—so far. Kent had just finished a steer wrestling demonstration, and his clothes were covered in dirt, there was a tear in the knee of his jeans, and one of his shirttails was hanging free.

Kent sighed and pushed his hat back to wipe sweat from his face with an old bandana. "Yeah." He angled his leg to get a better look at his knee. "Just a scratch."

"Even so," Eric said. He kneeled down to open the emergency field kit he'd placed near the arena entrance where he stood watch, and pulled out a package of antibacterial wipes. "Let me give it a quick cleaning. You'd be surprised how fast a minor cut untreated can turn into a major infection."

"Yes, Mom." Kent chuckled but hooked his boot onto the second railing of the arena fencing, giving Eric better access.

"He-Man," Eric joked. He pulled the torn material back from Kent's skin and started wiping away the dirt to get a better look at the cut. "So . . . is it just me or has Bridge been acting weird?"

Eric didn't look up, but he could feel the weight of Kent's stare on him. "Yeah. Something's going on with him. He'll tell us when he's ready."

Eric nodded, fighting back the urge to ask more questions, even though he knew Bridge was the only one he should be talking to about this. Except he had a feeling he knew exactly what was going on and some part of him didn't really want it confirmed.

He may have felt like he'd known the affable cowboys forever, that maybe he finally belonged somewhere, but in the back of his mind, he was still Disposable Eric. The kid whose parents said they loved him but kicked him to the curb; the new kid in the foster home who would always be the first one turned out if there was a rift between him and the established friends. If he let his original attraction to Bridge resurface any more than it had already, let something happen between them, he'd lose more than Bridge when it took its usual route south. He'd lose all of them because there was no way Marty and Kent would choose him over Bridge. No way anyone would choose him first.

Fuck, how did he let himself get in so deep with these guys? He knew better than to let his guard down and believe in fairy tales.

Before he could wander farther down Woe Is Me Road, commotion from the arena drew his attention. Eric turned in time to see a horse pull itself up from the ground, leaving its rider in the dirt. The riderless horse trotted off, shaking its head and snorting, clearly not impressed at having taken a fall, but the cowboy remained flat out on the ground. A split second later, Eric's stomach bottomed out when he recognized the cowboy. He swallowed back the sudden queasy lurch and shifted into professional mode. He grabbed his field kit, holding it under his arms to keep it closed rather than wasting time fastening the latches, and sprinted into the ring.

"Clear back," he barked at the cowboys who'd gathered at Bridge's side. Eric's heart pounded hard in his ears as he dropped to his knees beside the burly cowboy.

"Bridge." His voice cracked, and he heard the hint of panic in it. He took a deep breath, forcing himself to detach, forcing all his emotions into their assigned boxes so he could focus on his job. "Bridge, can you hear me?"

"Of course I can hear you." Bridge huffed. "Shit."

"Where are you hurt?" Eric began by visually searching for injuries, while pulling equipment from his kit.

"I'm not."

Eric inspected Bridge's face, pushing the long hair back from a furrowed brow. What wasn't covered in dirt looked pale, and his eyes were squeezed shut. "Then why are you still on the ground? And green?"

"Trying not to barf." Bridge's voice sounded weak, like he really was doing just that. Eric tried to shine his penlight into Bridge's eyes, to check for signs of concussion, but Bridge pushed his hand away and grunted. The sound more put-upon than in search of relief from injury.

"Are you going to be that kind of patient?" Eric said, keeping his tone even. People reacted all kinds of ways when they were hurt, but he didn't want Bridge to be one of the ones he had to fight in order to assess his injuries.

Bridge opened his eyes and looked up, searching Eric's. Whatever he saw there softened his expression, and warmth radiated outward, calming Eric when he was the one who was supposed to be calming the injured person he was attending to.

"If you're feeling nauseated, I'm worried you might have a concussion," he said, that trace of fear when he'd first seen Bridge on the ground creeping back into his voice.

"I'm sorry," Bridge said. His voice was quiet, laced with a note of vulnerability Eric had never heard from the man before. Not breaking his stare, Bridge lifted his left arm. "It's the blood. Somehow I got cut going down. Probably the cinch buckle or the edge of a conch."

Eric reached for the arm Bridge had indicated and carefully rolled up the torn shirtsleeve. On the inside of his forearm was a gash about three inches long. It didn't look deep enough to require stitches, just a good cleaning, butterfly strips, and a secure bandage. "That's it? No pain anywhere else?"

Bridge shook his head, and Eric watched him closely, pressing his fingertips to the cowboy's wrist, the pulse there strong and steady. Bridge stayed still and let Eric check his pupils this time, and then Eric gently palpated the ribs and abdomen for any signs of hemorrhaging or breaks. The whole time their gazes remained fixed on each other.

"Just a minor cut," Eric said. Satisfied Bridge was okay, his heart rate slowed, and he exhaled a relieved breath.

"It's bleeding," Bridge complained.

Eric relaxed further, chuckling at the man's insolent tone. "Well, yeah. That's what happens when you get a cut, genius, but it's not serious. I really think you're going to live to ride another day. Here, look."

"Can't." Bridge squeezed his eyes shut again.

"What do you mean you can't?"

Bridge groaned and then stage-whispered, "Blood! Freaks me out."

"Are you serious?" Eric leaned back on his heels, trying really hard to prevent the laughter from bubbling up but not succeeding. "Big, tough cowboy like you turns green over a little blood?"

"Oh, shut up," Bridge groused, cracking an eyelid to glare at Eric, but the hint of a smile teasing the edges of his mouth took any bite out of the words.

Eric shook his head. "You're so in the wrong business."

Bridge only huffed in response. Eric laid Bridge's arm carefully over his thigh, opened an antibacterial wipe, and began cleaning the wound. His gaze kept straying to Bridge's face, taking advantage of the man's closed eyes to study him freely. His lashes were long and a few shades darker than his hair, and there were faint freckles sprinkled across the bridge of his nose. His lips were pursed but held a healthy blush; the bottom one was fuller than the top. Golden fuzz covered his jaw, and Eric had the sudden urge to slide his tongue into the cleft of his chin.

He cleared his throat and focused on his task.

"Sit up, you big baby." He kept his tone light. "People are freaking that you might be seriously hurt."

Bridge did as he was told. "I like your accent," he said quietly, like a confession.

Eric paused, staring hard at the cloth in his hand because he couldn't look up into that handsome face right then. "Thank you," he said, his voice just as quiet, and went back to work. When the wound was clean, he quickly applied ointment then gauze, taped it up, and smacked Bridge on the shoulder when he was done.

"There. No more blood."

Bridge opened his eyes, and they locked on Eric's. There was a mix of embarrassment and gratitude in that rich, brown-eyed stare, but there was also . . . desire. Eric had the distinct feeling Bridge was about to lean over and kiss him, as though they were slowly inching toward each other by some unseen force. The fact that they were in the middle of a rodeo arena with an audience somehow seemed a distant concern. He licked his lips, and Bridge's gaze dropped to follow the movement. Then Bridge broke the connection by looking down at his arm and turning it over to inspect Eric's handiwork.

Eric released the breath that had gotten hung up in his throat and quickly put his supplies back in his kit.

"Thank you," Bridge said, his coy smile reaching down into Eric's chest and settling itself there. He was seeing a new side to Bridge today. The confident, playful side that fired up his engine and made him think—want—things he shouldn't, and then this. Vulnerable, shy, calling out to a part of Eric that wanted to wrap him up in his arms and protect him. Which was funny. No one could look at a man like Bridge and think he played any other role than protector. The guy was built like a brick house.

Eric stood and held out his hand. Bridge stared at him for a beat, then placed his hand in Eric's. Even through the leather glove Bridge wore, their touch made Eric's skin tingle. He pulled Bridge to his feet, which earned a round of applause from the small crowd. No one liked to see injuries at rodeos, whether it be the competitors, volunteers, or the roughstock, even though it was par for the course in the sport. A minor injury like Bridge's counted as a good day.

Bridge swayed briefly once he was vertical, his grip tightened on Eric, and he leaned forward. For the second time in as many minutes, Eric thought Bridge was about to go in for a kiss, and then he straightened up and stood steady. Bridge's hand slipped slowly from Eric's, fingertips lingering for a brief moment, and then it was gone.

A throat cleared. Loudly.

Preoccupied with Bridge's injury, Eric hadn't realized Marty had collected Bridge's horse and ridden up beside them, where he sat looking down with a teasing smile on his face. He held the reins out for Bridge.

"Don't even start," Bridge mumbled, shooting a warning glare at Marty, who laughed in response. He leaned down to collect his hat and dusted it off against his thigh before plopping it back on his head. He looked at Eric again and tapped a finger to the brim of his hat, then climbed up into the saddle and reined his horse back into the fray.

Just another day in the world of rodeo.

Like during the regular season, though with far less fanfare, Bridge and Kent set up a table for their traditional end-of-day card game while Marty doled out cold beers from a cooler that sat on the ground next to Marty's rig.

A hoot and holler drew their attention to Craig and Rowdy, a couple of old roughstock handlers they'd known as long as they'd been on the pro tour, who rounded the corner of the trailer.

"Been missing my poker games with you boys," Craig said, a huge smile splitting his weathered face, and he hugged and shook hands with them one by one. When he got to Tripp, he held on to his hand a little longer, leaning closer. "Real sorry 'bout what happened last year, Tripp. That weren't right."

"'Preciate it," Tripp said, a rough edge to his voice.

"Good to see you back, man," Rowdy said and pulled Tripp into a one-armed hug.

"All right!" Craig clapped his hands together, giving Bridge a start. "Enough jawing. Let's get down to emptying yer pockets."

Good-natured ribbing ensued while they tried to fit seven chairs around a four-chair table, when two new cowboys came around the back of the rig. Bridge immediately recognized Cory Ackerson, the rookie with a natural affinity for running pickup.

He also couldn't help notice the way Eric watched Cory stride past the card table, sizing him up, which immediately set his teeth on edge and darkened the edge of his vision.

"I'm sorry," Cory said when he stopped in front of Bridge. "I didn't mean to interrupt your game."

Bridge must have been glaring when he looked down at Cory, who was a whole head shorter than him with boots on, because an older, rougher-looking version of the young man stepped between them, his stance clearly protective. "I tried to tell him he could talk to you guys tomorrow, during official clinic hours, but he insisted." His expression was guarded, body language restrained, but he offered a hand. "Toby. Cory's brother."

"Nice to meet you," Bridge said, accepting the gesture and fighting back the grin that wanted to break free when Toby's grip tightened. Bridge understood the message, but he was one of the last people who needed the warning. He'd grown up doing the same thing where Marty was concerned.

"Toby." Marty shook his hand and smiled. "No worries. We haven't started yet."

"Cool!" Cory's smile was damn near blinding, and then he looked down at his boots for a second, like maybe he was nervous and needed to collect himself. When he lifted his gaze to look at the group, there was trepidation and naked hope glittering in his bright-blue eyes. "I, uh . . . I kind of wanted to talk to you guys about more than just pickup. Privately. I mean it's kind of obvious I'm gay, right? And I draw enough attention as it is, but I didn't want to bring on more during the sessions. So I was hoping I could talk to you tonight. I mean, if that's okay?" He flicked his eyes to Bridge. "I don't know if you're gay or not, Bridge, but everyone knows Marty is and you're his best friend, so . . . um . . . is it okay?"

Wow. Did the kid even take a breath?

"Of course it's okay," Marty said. "Grab a chair."

Bridge could only stand there for a second until his bearings reset themselves. Listening to Cory—and watching, because he was a hand talker—was like standing in the center of a mini tornado. The young man had a spark that was hard to ignore, no doubt about it. Bridge smiled. The kid's excitement was damn infectious, and he decided then that he liked the little greenhorn.

He reached for a chair and paused when his gaze met Eric's. Damn if there wasn't a hint of green flashing back in those captivating eyes. Encouraged, his smiled widened, and he raised an eyebrow. Eric frowned. The move was subtle, not something anyone would have seen if they'd hadn't been watching closely, but Bridge caught it. Eric dropped his stare to the table and started a determined shuffle of the cards.

Hopefully everyone would clear out early enough for him to have a private talk with Eric.

The night didn't progress quite as he'd hoped.

Cory had kept Bridge and Marty engaged as he fired off question after question, all the while peppering them with tales of his rodeo dreams and compliments on their prowess. Tripp had quickly been pulled into the conversation, and Toby had taken over his seat at the card table.

Bridge had found his gaze constantly drifting to the man who'd been playing a nightly role in his dreams. He'd hoped to get in on the game for at least one hand, but it was probably for the best he hadn't. He'd just have ended up losing all his coin, too distracted by Eric to focus on the game.

One by one, Kent, Craig, Rowdy, and Toby tossed their cards into a pile in the center of the table, grumbling at their losses while Eric grinned and scooped up his winnings. He shot a glance Bridge's way and winked.

"That's right," Bridge teased. "Enjoy the easy winnings. It won't last when I deal in next time."

"Whatever you say, pigeon," Eric shot back.

Bridge flipped him off, earning a round of laughter from the guys.

Cory looked between him and Eric, eyes wide with curious innocence, and then settled on Bridge. "What's pigeon mean?"

"Means he's a sucker," Eric answered, collecting chips and slotting them back in their plastic holder. "Don't be fooled into thinking he's a card shark."

"So says the kettle to the pot," Kent jibbed as he gathered the empty beer cans. "How much have you lost to him now?"

Eric looked at Kent in mock shock. "Whose side are you on, man?"

Laughter drifted off into the clear night sky, and Bridge stood, stretching his arms over his head to pop the kinks out of his spine from sitting so long. He'd changed into a T-shirt earlier, and now it rode up his torso, exposing a sliver of skin that Eric had definitely noticed. Bridge held still, letting Eric take in his fill while heat rose and spread under that stare—across his belly, up into his chest, and down into his groin. Damn it, this was no fantasy. He wanted Eric. In a bad way. Eric turned away first with a subtle shake of his head, and Bridge dropped his arms. Blood rushed back into his hands, leaving them feeling heavy and his head light.

That was when he noticed Kent watching him, a slight crease in his forehead signaling that his best friend was working something out in his mind. And Bridge had no doubt that *he* was the something.

"C'mon, Cory," Toby called out, drawing everyone's attention. "I think you've worn these guys out enough for one night."

Cory stood and hugged each of them, his hat falling off in the process. "Thanks, guys." He bent to pick it up and, with a bright smile, popped in back on his head without dusting it off. "I really appreciate y'all taking the time to talk with me and share your experience and know-how. I hope we get to hang out again and talk a lot more."

"Anytime," Bridge and Marty said in unison. Tripp nodded, and Toby rolled his eyes at them behind his brother.

When the card game was all packed up for the night and everyone had cleared out, Marty turned to Bridge. "Cory's adorable, but oh my God, can that boy talk."

Bridge couldn't help but laugh. "I know! It's like he doesn't even need to breathe between monologues."

"Kid done wore me out."

"Not too much, I hope," Tripp said and waggled his eyebrows. Kent groaned.

"And on that note . . ." Marty held out his hand for Tripp, who took it with an evil glint in his eyes. "See y'all at sunup."

Bridge watched as the pair disappeared into Marty's RV hand in hand, and then turned to Eric, who looked away quickly. He tossed his empty beer can into a box beside the cooler.

"Yeah," Eric said. "I'm out too. Been a long day."

Kent clapped Eric on the shoulder. "Later," he said and then went to do his usual final double check on the horses before turning in.

Bridge didn't really think about what he was doing, but before his brain caught up to his body, he'd closed the few feet between them and pulled Eric into a hug. Maybe he'd just meant it as a quick good-night-buddy one-armed-back-pat kind of thing, but when the burning heat of Eric's hands settled on his hips, he squeezed a bit tighter, held on a little longer, and then did what he'd been wanting to the day before: he lowered his head into the crook of Eric's neck and inhaled deeply. For as long as he lived, he would forever associate the smell of spice and oranges with Eric.

His voice was deeper, a touch gravelly when he said, "Later, dude."

He loosened his hold, and Eric stepped back, putting a safe distance between them. There was unmistakable desire in his eyes, but something else lurked in the background that didn't seem to fit. Fear? Pain? Definitely a sense of distance rising between them.

Bridge opened his mouth, but Eric cut him off before he had a chance to form a single word. "Good night, Bridge." Without waiting for a response, he turned and disappeared around the back of Marty's trailer.

*What the hell was that?*

Off-center but amped up, Bridge turned to find Kent watching him intently and mentally groaned. He shoved his hands into his pockets.

"What?"

Kent leaned back against the trailer and hooked his thumbs in his belt loops. "You know those times me and Marty asked if you had something to tell us? You know we were always just joking around, right?"

Bridge nodded when it was clear Kent was waiting for acknowledgment.

"Well," Kent continued. "Now I'm asking for real."

Bridge sighed, took his hat off, and ran a hand through his hair. "Yeah, I have something to tell you guys. But not yet. Okay?" He settled his hat back in place. "I'm going to take a walk along the river before turning in."

Kent nodded, flashed a warm smile, and then turned and climbed up into their RV.

Bridge looked to the sky and sighed. Tomorrow. Tomorrow he would get Eric alone and see where things might stand.

# CHAPTER FOUR

Halfway through the second day of the clinic, Eric was finishing up lunch at the picnic table with Bridge. Marty and Tripp had left early to "take care of a couple of things" again before the afternoon sessions started, and Kent had eaten earlier and was off talking shop with some fellow steer wrestlers.

Eric looked up and met Bridge's stare across the table. The wheels were clearly turning in the man's head, and there was a glint of humor in his expression. He reminded Eric of a big cat readying to pounce. He shifted slightly in his seat, wanting to be the mouse as much as he didn't. "I'm afraid to ask."

"I want to teach you to ride," Bridge said, lifting the soda cup to his lips.

"Oh, believe me," Eric said, pitching his voice low. "I know how to ride quite well."

Bridge choked on the sip he'd just taken, his eyes widening while a flush spread over the swells of his cheekbones. Endearing, Eric thought, how Bridge could manage embarrassed and turned on at the same time. But also telling how quick Bridge had picked up on his meaning.

"A horse, stud," Bridge said, his voice ragged from the reversed bubbles, and reached for a napkin to wipe the spilled cola from his chin, pooled right in that little cleft Eric kept wanting to slide his tongue into. "I can't believe you've been hanging around the rodeo this long and haven't ever ridden a horse."

Eric shrugged, eyes following Bridge's hand as he wiped. "I'm here for the cowboys."

Bridge shook his head, furrowing his brow, and a disapproving frown pushed the corners of his mouth downward. "Seriously, dude. A cowboy without a horse is like a PB&J without the J."

"I'll have you know, there are a lot of cowboys in New York who don't have horses."

"Yeah, like that naked guy who plays guitar in Times Square? Please." Bridge rolled his eyes and tossed the soiled napkin on the table beside his plate. "I saw him on YouTube. He's no cowboy. Nice legs, though."

Eric raised his eyebrows. How many straight guys did he know who said things like that? Answer: none. "Seriously? You were checking him out?"

"I can appreciate an attractive man," Bridge said. There was a playful note in his voice, but there was no teasing in the heated, promising look he leveled at Eric. It was another one of those bells-and-whistles stares that didn't need words to indicate what it meant, and his pulse quickened in response.

God, he needed to stop noticing things like that. It would lead to no good for him. Either he'd let himself believe Bridge wasn't straight only to find out he really was and he'd be made a fool. Or he'd find out Bridge was gay, and interested in him, which would be worse. He knew better than to believe someone like Bridge would want him—at least not for more than just sex. Jeremy had made that painfully clear when he'd chosen another over him, even after professing his undying love. Like Ron before him, who Eric had also foolishly believed had loved him.

Nope, he couldn't go there again. As long as he kept his heart locked down, no one would ever be able to hurt him again, and if it were Bridge . . . the heartbreak would be devastating.

Eric broke the connection first, needing a distraction to keep his bearings. Friends he could do. Harmless, flirty fun he could do. But that would have to be their line in the sand.

He grabbed a salted potato chip off his plate and waved it in Bridge's direction as if it were some kind of shield. "Okay, fine. Teach me to ride a horse." He paused to basically inhale the chip. "But can we start on the coin-operated ones in front of the grocery stores? They're close enough to the ground that even if I do manage to fall off, I won't get hurt."

Bridge raised his eyebrows. "And just yesterday you wanted to learn bull riding?"

"Well, I'd start on a mechanical one, right?"

Bridge scowled. "No ponies or mechanical horses." Then he leaned forward and his voice dropped, sounding as smooth as twelve-year-old whiskey tasted. "The real deal is what I've got for you."

"Are you flirting with me again?" He'd meant the question to come off light and teasing, but his rough whisper startled even him. Against his better judgment, he had to admit how much he liked the way Bridge flirted with him, how much he was starting to enjoy it, and look forward to it. It was just harmless teasing between friends, after all. No harm, no foul. Right?

He could do that.

Bridge smiled, and then his expression turned serious. "So." He leaned back. "In all the time we've known you, you've never said much about your life in New York. Why is that?"

Well, that wasn't at all where he'd expected the conversation to go. He'd so much rather tempt fate with their growing sexual innuendo than talk about his past. He took a long drink of his iced tea. "Not much to tell."

Bridge snagged the last chip off Eric's plate and dipped it into a leftover dollop of mustard on his own. "How old are you?"

Eric watched with rapt attention as Bridge opened his mouth, slid the rippled chip into his mouth, and bit down, his tongue snaking out to swipe the trace of yellow condiment that clung to his lip.

Eric had to clear his throat, and even then, his words crawled out slow and spent sounding. "The dreaded thirty."

"So after thirty years of living, there's nothing to tell? I don't believe that for a second. What about family? Brothers and sisters?"

"Don't have any."

Bridge leaned back, eyebrows raised. "As much as I'd like to think you were sent from heaven, I don't think you just dropped here last year, fully formed."

"Aww." Looking for a deflection, Eric folded his hands and rested his chin on them, giving Bridge his best dreamy eyes and fluttering his lashes. "Who knew you were such a romantic?"

Bridge lowered his head, but the brim of his hat wasn't wide enough to hide the blush that spread over his cheeks. Confident and shy—why that blend intrigued Eric so much, he couldn't say, but the more he discovered about Bridge, the more he wanted to discover. Which was damn dangerous thinking, and he needed to get off that train wreck in the making.

"Shut up and tell me your story," Bridge groused.

Eric inhaled deeply, held it, then expelled a long breath. "Parents dumped me in foster care. Got bounced around to a lot of homes." At Bridge's look of concern, he added, "No, I was never abused or neglected." *Just not wanted.* "As soon as I was old enough, I left the boroughs for Albany. Decided I wanted to help people, went to school and got my paramedic degree. Ended up covering at a rodeo in Greenwich and fell in love with the whole atmosphere. Fell hard for a cowboy who turned out to be in the closet and only using me to get his rocks off when his wife was out of town. Thought the opposite coast would make a nice change of scenery since nothing rooted me to New York, and here I am."

Bridge stared at him for a long moment, his eyes searching, expression unreadable, lips pressed into a flat line but not hard enough to turn them white around the edges. Eric got the impression he was cataloging everything he'd just learned.

"Someday you'll tell me the whole story."

Eric opened his mouth to tell him that *was* the whole story, but Bridge glanced at his watch and jumped up. "Time to get back to it."

Eric stood and gathered his empty lunch wrappers, grateful that particular conversation was over. Hopefully never to be revived.

"Don't forget, we have a riding lesson after classes today," Bridge said. Then he winked and turned toward the parking area and his horses, long legs eating up the ground in graceful strides.

Eric shook his head. *What the hell am I getting myself into?*

"Use your knees!" Bridge fought back the urge to laugh, but it wasn't easy. Not when Rosie started jogging and Eric stuck his legs straight out, gripped the horn so hard his knuckles turned white, and bounced around in the saddle while the reins hung loose and ineffective.

"Why did I let you talk me into this?" Eric shouted from the far end of a small clearing behind the trailers. He'd refused to learn how to ride in the arena where anyone could see, even though most people were tending to their animals or had left the grounds for early dinners. "This animal is about to rattle all the teeth out of my head."

"That *animal's* name is Rosie, and she has the smoothest gait of all my horses. She also has the sweetest personality or you'd be on your ass in the dirt right now, flailing around in the saddle like that."

"I'm not flailing."

Bridge leaned back against a light pole at the edge of the clearing. "Sure looks it from here."

"And I'm not supposed to *be* a cowboy," Eric argued and pulled the reins back to slow Rosie to a walk. "Just love them."

*Just love them.*

The words bounced around Bridge's mind, their echo growing rather than fading, but he pushed them away and cleared his throat. "I'll make a cowboy out of you yet. You'll see."

Eric snorted and reined Rosie toward Bridge at a casual mosey. "Nobody has that much patience," he said when horse and rider came to a halt in front of Bridge.

He stared up at Eric, caught in those purple-infused blue eyes he found so entrancing, and realized that no matter what may or may not come of them as a couple, he'd do anything and everything he could for the man.

He smiled, lowered his voice, and hoped Eric picked up on the promise behind his words. "I've got all the patience in the world for you, stud."

Eric tilted his head slightly but didn't say anything.

"Here." Bridge stepped to Rosie's right side and adjusted Eric's foot. "Heel down, toe back, so it aligns with your knee. Reins in your left hand; hold them just over the horn. Not too much tension; not too slack. Hold the extra rein in your right hand and rest it on your thigh." He placed Eric's hand where he'd instructed, then let his own rest for a second on the hard muscle there. He moved his hands to Eric's hips, guiding them back. "Hips under your center of gravity. Gives you a deeper seat so you don't go bouncing out of the saddle."

Eric grinned. "You just want to feel up my ass."

"Couldn't help myself," Bridge said, then winked and stepped back, smacking Rosie lightly on the rump. "Now walk."

Eric slanted a dubious look down at him, while Rosie responded immediately, with a swish of her long flaxen tail.

"Now squeeze with your knees, drop your hips, and ask her to jog."

Eric followed his instructions, tapping Rosie into an easy jog with his heels, and sat back in the saddle like a seasoned cowboy. "There. Now you just need a hat and proper boots, and you'll look like the real deal."

"This is much more comfortable," Eric agreed, and Bridge didn't miss the note of excitement in his voice. A little swell of pride rose up in his chest.

"Ready to try loping?"

"Is that like galloping?"

"Close. The gallop is a four-beat gait all about speed and short distance; loping is a slower, three-beat gait that can be maintained longer because it's more controlled. English riders call it a canter."

"Wow, I had no idea there was so much more to it than get on and ride."

Bridge crossed his arms. "You'd better be teasing me right now."

"Okay." Eric raised a hand in surrender, laughing. "Next gear, oh wise one."

Bridge snorted and shook his head. "Lean forward in the saddle slightly and apply light pressure to her sides with your lower legs. Click your tongue too, if want, but horses are highly sensitive and respond better to physical commands. Especially working and rodeo horses because there's so much noise and activity going on, they might not hear you."

Rosie shifted into a smooth lope, and Eric started to bounce forward. "Roll your hips back into the seat. Grip with your knees. Good!"

"I like this much better than trotting!" Eric shouted over his shoulder after he'd settled into the saddle.

"It's jogging!" Bridge laughed. "When you're ready to stop, remember to lean back slightly and pull the reins just until you feel tension. Rosie doesn't need any more direction than that."

Eric loped back toward Bridge and brought the chestnut mare to a halt, mere feet from him. The smile Eric bestowed on him felt like the very sun itself leaned down from the sky and kissed him. Damn, he had it bad.

"Just like an old hand."

Eric swung his right leg over Rosie's back to dismount, swaying the second his feet hit the ground. He grabbed hold of the saddle pommel and cantle to keep himself upright.

Bridge laughed. *Greenhorns.* "Well, almost an old hand. Don't worry. You'll get the hang of that before too long."

He stepped behind Eric, fighting the urge to wrap his arms around the man's trim waist and nuzzle the side of his neck, run a tongue along the corded muscle there, lick and taste and—

Eric turned and looked up at him, smile still in full-blinding mode. "Thank you. I really didn't think I'd enjoy that as much as I did."

Bridge nodded, lowering his voice as if he were sharing a secret. "Then we'll do it again. Go for a ride together."

"I'd like that," Eric said, his voice pitched down to match.

Eric held his gaze, and the light in those deep eyes darkened, drawing Bridge in. The gentle breeze shifted and that arousing scent he'd come to identify with Eric mixed with leather and horse and spring bloom, teasing his senses, feeding his arousal. In the distance, he could hear the steady gurgle of the river, and closer, he could almost hear his own heartbeat.

He licked his lips, and Eric's gaze dropped to follow the swipe of his tongue. *Holy good God . . .* "Listen, I—"

The sound of a throat clearing nearby brought an abrupt halt to the confession he'd been on the verge of making. Bridge stepped back, disappointment and relief warring in his chest, and looked over Rosie's withers to see Kent standing a few feet away at the edge of the clearing.

"Looking good in the saddle there, Eric," Kent said.

"Thanks. I honestly never thought I'd find myself actually riding." Eric slid a quick glance at Bridge. "A horse."

Bridge groaned and shook his head, then laughed at Kent's confused expression, only to laugh harder when Kent widened his eyes, having got it. A blush crept over his cheeks. "O-kay," he said, embarrassment threading through his voice. "Eric, the boss lady is looking for you. Something about not having an on-call ambulance available for tomorrow."

"Shit." Eric turned to Bridge, a question in his eyes.

"I'll take care of Rosie. Do what you need to."

"Thanks again. For the lesson," Eric said quietly.

"Anytime." Bridge smiled, holding Eric's stare a moment longer, then Eric turned and jogged toward the main clubhouse. When Eric was out of sight, Bridge turned to Kent. It was clear from the intent way Kent watched him that he was out of free passes. "Go on. Spill it," he said, resigned.

Kent didn't hesitate. "You know I'm the first to say go for it if you're attracted to someone, right? I love you like a brother and only want you to be happy, no matter who that's with. But . . ." He paused, and the note of warning in his tone was unmistakable. "If this is just a curiosity thing about being with men, in general, don't experiment with Eric. He's been a good friend to us all, and I'd hate to see him get fucked over."

Bridge jerked back. Kent may as well have punched him in the gut. "Dude. You know I'd never do that."

"I know you never would in your heart or your mind"—Kent's tone softened—"but I also know your dick doesn't give a shit. If you find yourself in a hot and heavy corner, you'll go with it, consequences be damned. So I'm just saying, if it's curiosity, find someone else. Okay?"

Bridge scowled and turned away. "Okay. Got it," he snapped, his voice gruff. He resented that Kent thought he could toy with Eric like that. Yes, he'd been worried about whether or not he was really attracted to Eric in particular or if, for some strange reason, it was long-forgotten desires that had risen to the surface again that he wanted to explore. But in spending more time with Eric, he knew the answer to that now, without a doubt. He was attracted to Eric and only Eric. In every way.

But at the same time, what else could Kent think? Bridge hadn't brought everyone else up to speed yet. Kent didn't know how long he'd been working this attraction through—didn't even know he'd explored before. Bridge sighed. First he had to talk to Eric.

# CHAPTER
## FIVE

L ater that night, after the poker game and another Cory visit had wrapped, and after Marty and Tripp had made another quick exit, Eric took his time putting away the last of the cards and chips.

"Okay, ladies. I'm calling this day done too," Kent said. He leveled a warning glare at Bridge, who was chucking beer cans into a box on the ground by the cooler, and then pulled the door to their RV open. "Don't stay up all night talking about boys."

The metal door clapped shut behind him, and then it was just the two of them and the suddenly-too-still night.

"What was that look?" Eric walked over to toss the empty beer can he'd been holding on to like a security blanket into the box at Bridge's feet.

Bridge shrugged. "Nothing." He half turned, like he was about to head out for the night, even though he'd told Eric earlier that he wanted to talk to him after the game. A part of Eric didn't want Bridge to leave yet, but the idea of what Bridge might want to talk about had his nerves strung tight. Bridge shoved his hands in his pockets and settled those beautiful brown eyes on him.

"Got something I want to ask you." He looked a bit uncomfortable, like he really didn't want to ask but was forging ahead anyway.

Eric nodded. "Okay." He wasn't sure he wanted to answer the question he knew was coming either. It definitely had to do with the looks and innuendo Bridge had been throwing at him lately, but nervous energy radiated from the man in waves and Eric felt a rising need to ease his anxiety.

"Look, I hope this doesn't freak you out." Bridge took off his hat, ran a hand through his unruly blond locks, and then gripped the brim of the hat in both hands, fidgeting with the felt edges instead of putting it back on. Trepidation danced in the depths of his gaze, but his eyes remained on Eric. "I know you don't think I'm gay. No one does. Well, maybe not so much lately, but . . . if you thought I was, would you . . ." Bridge swallowed audibly. "Would you be interested in me? That way?"

*Ka-boom.* Didn't get much more point-blank than that.

He searched Bridge's eyes—open, honest, scared. So many emotions gathered there, but the one standing out the most was hope. Gay or not, Bridge seemed genuinely interested in him. And what could he say? Hell yes, he was interested right back, but that didn't erase the fear. When Bridge realized Eric wasn't worth it—which he would, just like everyone else had his whole life—he'd lose not only Bridge's friendship, but Marty, Tripp and Kent's, too.

"Bridge. Um . . ."

"Shit, now I've made you uncomfortable." Bridge looked away, and Eric's chest clenched. "I'm sorry. I didn't mean—"

Before he knew it, he'd reached out and wrapped his hand lightly around Bridge's bare wrist, the skin there warm and firm, sending electric charges up Eric's arm. "No, no. We're good. I swear. It's just . . ."

"Just what?"

Eric didn't miss the hopeful undertone in Bridge's question, the way he seemed to lean forward ever so slightly.

"It's just that . . ." Eric chewed his lip, trying to corral his thoughts, but the heat that radiated into his palm where it connected with Bridge's bare skin kept interfering with his thought process. "You aren't gay. And we're good friends."

"Well . . . do I have to be gay to be interested?" A hint of a smile lifted one side of Bridge's mouth. "And don't they say best friends make the best lovers?"

*Holy shit.* This was not going to go easy. Eric cleared his throat—twice—and dropped his hand from Bridge's wrist. He couldn't touch the sexy cowboy and think clearly at the same time. "Generally, men who are attracted to other men are gay . . ."

"But some men are attracted to both men and women."

"Bisexual," Eric said.

Bridge shook his head and made a face—annoyed, impatient, amused, and completely adorable. "Closer, but how about if we just say I'm attracted to you?"

Bridge studied him for a moment that seemed to go on for far too long. Long enough for Eric to imagine sparks shooting between them. Though that was probably from the fading embers of the small campfire they'd had going earlier, he told himself.

"*Are* you saying you're attracted to me?" The words drifted out on a whisper so soft, Eric could barely hear his own voice. A little flicker of hope lit in the depths of his mind, but he forced it back into the dark.

Bridge nodded, and his smile widened. "Definitely."

"But . . ." Eric's thoughts warred with each other, one part jumping for joy and another looking for the closest window to jump out of and run. "Since when?"

"Since you came to the hospital to check up on Marty last year."

"What?" Eric's voice cracked, and his eyebrows rose so high they seemed to be trying to weave into his hairline.

Bridge looked down at his feet, kicked at the dirt with the toe of his boot, his smile turning shy. "Well, I didn't really know what was going on then. Lots of feelings I hadn't felt in a really long time. Only stronger. But then over the winter, I started having these dreams . . ." He glanced up and the heat in his eyes singed the surface of Eric's skin. "Really erotic dreams, and that's when—"

"Stop." Eric raised a hand and took a step back. "You don't just suddenly realize you're gay at twenty-five—"

"Eight. But thank you."

He groaned. "Whatever. Being attracted to the same sex is something you pretty much know from a young age."

"It's not sudden, and I'm not gay. I like women too. And you."

Eric dropped his chin to his chest and sighed. "Bridge . . . you're killing me here."

"I've been with a man before." Bridge's voice was quiet, conspiratorial sounding. "Once, in college, and it was seriously hot. You're the first person I've ever told, by the way. But then I met this girl and just figured I was straight, mostly, so everyone else thought the same thing. I met a few guys over the years that I thought were hot, but none made me want to act on it." Bridge took a step closer, eating into the space Eric had put between them. "And then you came along, and you make me want to act on that. You're all I can think about."

Bridge tossed his cowboy hat onto the cooler by the trailer and took another step forward. "Tell me I'm not alone here."

*You're not!*

He looked up into Bridge's eyes, at the naked desire he saw there, the fervent anticipation. "It's not that. We're friends. Good friends, and I value that too much to risk losing it, losing all of you guys, if we cross that line and it doesn't work." He swallowed hard, trying to ignore the dimming flare of hope in that gold-flecked gaze. "And you know, like, you don't move in with your best friend from high school because that's the fastest way to destroy your friendship. So getting romantically involved with your best friend is kind of the same deal."

Bridge frowned. "Kent and I bought a ranch together when we finished college. It's been six years. And we've been best friends, hung out pretty much every day of our lives, since we were in diapers."

*Okay, maybe that wasn't the best example.* "So, you're the exception to the rule."

Bridge smiled. Slow and seductive, confusing the signals in Eric's brain almost as effortlessly as touching him had. "No reason we can't be an exception to the rule too."

"But it's still not a good idea because we're good friends, and far too often, a sure way to fuck up a good friendship is to, well . . . *fuck* it up."

"Okay. I'll give you that, in some cases. But sometimes best friends make the best roommates, like Kent and me. So it stands to reason that sometimes best friends can also make the best lovers." Bridge took another step, putting himself so fully in Eric's space that the heat radiating off the man's solid frame drifted over him like a summer-morning mist. Then the expression on Bridge's face changed, closed somehow. His eyes hardened, and he retreated a couple of steps. "Sure. I get it." He bent to collect his hat and settled it back on his head. "Some friendships are too valuable to fuck up."

"Yeah." Eric's chest constricted, his lungs squeezing tighter instead of relaxing in relief. That was what he wanted, right? To stay friends, and only friends. So why did Bridge agreeing to let it go gouge his insides like this?

Bridge moved to walk around him, and Eric fought harder than he'd thought he'd have to not to reach out for the man. Bridge kicked dirt onto the last glowing ember in the fire pit, ensuring it was completely out. Eric frowned. Why couldn't his attraction to Bridge be so easily doused?

When Bridge turned around, Eric was still standing there, watching him. His face in shadow, but somehow clearer. The more Eric had argued about not wanting to risk their friendship, the more he saw it for the lie it was. Eric's eyes, his body language, told a different story. Something had Eric spooked, that much he could tell, but the idea that he wouldn't even give them a shot rankled Bridge. Maybe it was a bad idea, but what if it wasn't? And right now, the way Eric stood there looking at him like a steak he wanted to dig into did nothing to convince Bridge they could ever stay just friends.

And then Eric's tongue snaked out and ran along his top lip. The action seemed more absent than deliberate, but it was enough for Bridge.

"Goddamn it, Eric." He reached out and grabbed the front of Eric's shirt, pulling him closer until their chests bumped together and he froze. He stared into Eric's eyes, searching for a sign that he'd gone too far, already crossed the imaginary friends-only line, but all he saw was his own need reflected back. Eric's breath ghosted over his mouth, his cheek, and sent a rush of burning desire to all points. Bad idea or not, he didn't care. He'd wanted Eric for too long.

Bridge groaned, but it felt more like a growl with the way it tore a path through his throat. "You make me want to fuck it all up."

Before Eric could respond, he dipped his head down and claimed Eric's mouth. The first touch sent a jolt of electricity through him, igniting every nerve ending in his body. But Eric remained still, unresponsive, and for a heart-stopping second that seemed to stretch forever, Bridge worried that he really did just cross a line and fuck everything up. He began to pull back, to plead some kind of temporary insanity or a glitch in the time-space continuum to try to rewind and leave everything as it had been, when Eric's arms snaked around Bridge's waist and held him, tight. A rumbling moan drifted between them, and Eric pressed his tongue to the seam of Bridge's lips. He opened, and Eric slipped inside.

Bridge's dreams hadn't come close to the reality of kissing Eric Palmer. Not by a country mile. There was no way he could have imagined the silky-smooth feel of Eric's warm lips, the way day-old scruff brushed over his skin, the strong, wet slide of Eric's tongue as it dueled with his, and holy hell, their tongues dueled! Never had he been on the receiving end of such an aggressive kiss, felt such demand to be so . . . consumed, so needed, and then there was the taste. Heady and spicy and it shot through his veins like liquid fire.

This. This was what he'd wanted. This was what he'd been looking for all his life. He knew in that moment, without a single doubt, he was head over heels for Eric, and there was no going back. Not now. Not ever.

Eric broke the kiss first and stepped back, lips glistening in the low light of the rodeo grounds, chest heaving. Tiny gossamer clouds puffed out into the space between them as their heated breaths collided with the cool night air. "You're not alone here." His thickly accented voice was low and ragged.

"Knew it." Bridge smiled, forcing himself to stay still even as his skin felt tight on his bones and his fingers itched to pull Eric back against him. He didn't know what to do next, only knew that he wanted more. More kisses like that, more of that unique flavor, more of that lean body notched so perfectly to his. They may have just crossed a line, but fuck if anything had ever felt more right than Eric in his arms.

The door of Marty's RV banged open, and they both jumped, Eric taking another step back. Heat infused Bridge's cheeks, and for a second, he felt like a kid who'd been caught up to no good. Which was maybe not too far off.

"Hey, B." Marty hung out the doorframe, seeming oblivious to the tension vibrating in the air like a visible force field around him and Eric. "Is there any ice left? Tripp's leg is bugging him."

"Yeah." Bridge walked over to the cooler where he'd tossed his hat and put it back on. "Give me just a minute."

"Thanks, dude," Marty said, and then disappeared back inside.

Eric ran a hand over his shorn head, and Bridge followed the motion with his eyes, wanting the hand to be his, to feel the short hair under against his palm. He looked up to the sky and pulled his bottom lip into his mouth. Stars scattered in organized chaos across the black sheet of night. Then he dropped his gaze back to meet Eric's. "That was the best kiss I've ever had in my entire life."

Eric smiled then, more dazzling than even those damn stars. He stepped forward, pressed a chaste kiss to Bridge's mouth, and then backed out of reach before Bridge could trap him in his embrace again. "Get ice for Tripp. I'll see you tomorrow."

Bridge nodded, smiling so wide he thought his whole face might split in half. "Tomorrow."

# CHAPTER SIX

E ric hadn't been able to sleep more than a few hours but still managed to find himself wide-awake well before the sun rose or any of the other campers on the rodeo grounds began to stir. He'd been too amped up thinking about Bridge, replaying the kiss they'd shared, imagining how things could be between them, dreaming for something he knew he couldn't ever hope to hold on to. Not for long anyway. Usually only long enough for the inevitable parting to destroy what tiny threads of hope he still clung to.

Laced with those old, deep-seated fears were brand-new ones about the man who was burrowing into his subconscious. Bridge may have experimented with men once before, but he hadn't been with a man since. How much could Eric trust that it hadn't been anything more than a good old college try and maybe now Bridge just wanted to take a little trip down memory lane?

Either way, sooner or later Bridge would see what everyone else had seen: that there was something inherently wrong with Eric. Why else would everyone he had ever loved, or had thought had loved him, kick him to the curb? He wanted what Bridge and his friends had—that unconditional camaraderie, that belonging, that confidence that he was wanted and loved. But the more he wished and prayed for love, the more elusive it seemed to become. All he knew of that mysterious emotion was pain. Every time he'd let himself believe that maybe this time would be different was when it'd all come crashing down again.

But history couldn't keep repeating itself his whole life, could it? Marty, Bridge, Kent, and even Tripp, now that he was back in the fold, had somehow managed to weave him seamlessly into the thick fabric of their circle when he wasn't looking. And he had to admit those threads felt stronger than any he'd tried to hold on to before.

But what exactly made him think this time really *would* be any different?

The answer came fast: Bridge Sullivan.

The man was solid. A rock in the eye of the storm. No matter what happened, he stood by his friends. He made sure everyone around him was happy, and when Bridge looked at him with those enchanting dark eyes, he found himself falling deeper and deeper into their soothing depths. Not to mention he was one of the most beautiful men Eric had ever laid eyes on. Who wouldn't find themselves diving down the rabbit hole for someone like him?

But then there was the whole reawakened-interest-in-men-at-twenty-eight-years-old part.

He huffed and kicked back the bed covers.

Could he let himself believe, hope, that it wasn't just temporary curiosity? He didn't want to be an experiment for Bridge, and he didn't want to let his hopes cloud reality. Bridge was one of the best friends he'd ever had. All of them were. Deep down he knew none of them would deliberately hurt him, especially Bridge, who looked out for everyone, but that wasn't a guarantee against losing them all. It was, however, a guarantee that this time the end would crush him forever. So it really was best not to cross that friends-only line. At least no more than they already had. Save the mess and stay friends. Let Bridge find someone else to satisfy his curiosity.

A little green ember of jealousy dug its roots into the back of his mind at the thought of someone else kissing Bridge, someone else burrowed into that melt-worthy embrace, fingers that weren't his fisting in that lush blond hair . . .

No. If anyone was going to reteach Bridge the joys of gay sex, who better than a friend who truly cared about him? Someone who wouldn't do anything to hurt him, make him do anything he didn't want to, or put undue expectations on him.

*Someone like me.*

He'd been compartmentalizing his life as long as he could remember, so no reason he couldn't do that here too. It wasn't like Bridge would want him for more than a fling anyway, so why not help a friend discover—or rediscover—himself?

As long as he kept his heart and his elusive dreams locked down.

A whisper of dissent tickled at his thoughts, but he pushed it away.

Not able to stay in bed any longer, he rolled down from the tiny sleep space of his camper and pulled on his work clothes. Before anything else, a strong cup of coffee was on order. He grabbed a can of grounds from the cupboard above a two-burner stove top, dumped a measured amount into a single-cup coffeemaker sitting on the foot-wide counter, and pressed the On button. He sat down on the tiny couch beside the square of kitchen while his coffee brewed and pulled the shade back from the narrow window.

He'd parked his truck so it faced his friends' two equine-RV combo rigs. Those things were huge, and he marveled at how much money it took just to follow the circuit, let alone compete, especially when the winnings were lean and so many cowboys walked away empty-handed at the end of the day. It was definitely a sport born of pure love and tradition, and it didn't take much to see the draw. He himself had been lured by the history and fantasy of the Wild West—and the rugged men who'd tamed it.

The door to the RV that Bridge and Kent shared swung open, and Eric held his breath when the man who'd had him tossing and turning half the night stepped out into the brisk morning and stretched his arms over his head, breath gusting out to briefly cloud his face. The cowboy's gaze immediately homed in on Eric's camper and locked on him. He couldn't have looked away even if he tried. Fuck, that man was gorgeous. Bridge smiled and tapped his forefinger to the brim of his hat—another thing Eric fucking loved when Bridge did it—then turned, giving his ass a little shake before going about getting his horses fed and groomed for the day.

"I'm so screwed," he mumbled, unable to stop from smiling.

There was no denying it. He wanted what Bridge was offering, even as doubt gnawed at the back of his mind that it would be a one-time thing, or worse, bring about the end of the only time he'd ever felt he truly belonged somewhere. But he could be what Bridge needed him to be for however long that might be. Wouldn't be the first time.

Coffee brewed, he poured the steaming hot liquid into a travel mug and put on a second cup. When that one was ready, he filled another mug and left his camper.

Bridge had his back to him when Eric walked quietly between the trailers. He was grooming Rosie, the horse Eric had ridden yesterday, who was tethered to a steel ring soldered to the trailer's frame.

Eric stopped, taking a minute to admire the big cowboy before making his presence known. His hair was longer than most cattlemen's and hung in relaxed waves over the collar of a red Western shirt emblazoned with the logo of the pro-rodeo tour's main sponsor in white across the back. As Bridge reached to brush Rosie's neck, the shirt stretched flat against supple, delineated muscle, and Eric's fingers twitched to trace the hard lines of the solid lats that led to a trim waist and lower. Bridge's ass was a thing of beauty. Well-worn Wranglers hugged firm globes, which were further highlighted by rawhide chaps wrapped around thick, strong thighs.

*Caution, meet wind.*

He swallowed. Or maybe he groaned aloud, because Bridge turned then. That brown-eyed stare burned a sizzling path on Eric's skin as it slid down the length of his body and back up to settle on his mouth.

"Mornin.'" Bridge's voice was barely above a whisper, but the rough edge to it sent a charge of electric arousal coursing through Eric.

Then the man smiled. A smile so full of life and genuine joy that the warmth of it wrapped around Eric, dousing all of his doubts and fears. As though he'd just been blessed by the very heavens themselves.

He cleared his throat but couldn't pull his eyes from Bridge's. "Mornin.'" Remembering the coffee in his hands, he held up a mug and stepped forward. "Brought java."

"My savior." Bridge reached for the mug, and when his fingers brushed against Eric's, the skin where they met ignited, sending a sizzle of excitement rushing up his arm. One side of Bridge's mouth rose into a knowing smile as he slowly pulled his hand away and lifted the mug. Eric watched, mesmerized by those red lips closing over the lip of the cup. Bridge's eyelids dropped, and a deep, satisfied moan followed the sip he took. The sensual growl went straight to Eric's groin, and he had to look away. Maybe if he focused on the scratched paint of the trailer or the dent that looked like a horse had put a hoof to it, he could keep thinking with his brain rather than his body. Then Bridge stepped closer, drawing Eric's attention back, and leaned down to kiss him. Not the passionate want-you-right-fucking-now kiss of the previous night, but more of an affectionate see-you-after-work-sweetheart kiss, which seemed, by turns, far more intimate and much scarier. "Thank you."

Eric stared up at Bridge, unable to speak while his mind tried to reengage itself, and saw the moment Bridge wanted more, when the golden-flecked brown of his eyes shifted to a darker hue. Bridge took another step forward, until their chests touched, and kissed him again. Nothing chaste about this meeting of mouths, especially when Eric parted his lips and invited Bridge's tongue inside to play. He angled his head to deepen the kiss, taking as much of the cowboy as he could, savoring the bitter tang of coffee mixed with the essence of the man, his senses dancing in delight. Bridge slid one arm around his waist, and he barely registered the horse brush Bridge was still holding as it dug into his back.

Eric sunk into the man. It had been a long time since he'd been with anyone, a long time since he'd been wrapped in strong arms, and his whole body cried for more. He reached around and cupped Bridge's ass with his free hand, pulling him closer, tighter, trying to merge them into one, to lose himself in that welcoming heat. The outline of Bridge's swelling cock against his navel threatened to short-circuit his thoughts, but a loud equine snort and stomp of a hoof snapped him back to reality.

*Shit.*

He broke the kiss and took a step back, slamming the brakes on the runaway car that was his libido. They might be hidden from public view, the way the two rigs were parked like a shield, but now was not the time or place.

"I want more of that," Bridge said, his voice a low rasp and his eyes a blazing fire.

"I do too." Eric adjusted his jeans in search of a little breathing room, drawing Bridge's stare, and with it a flare of heat that fanned through the length of his cock. "Obviously." He fought down the rush. He needed to think clearly, set the ground rules before things got out of hand. "But remember what I said last night about fucking things up? I"—*I'm afraid*—"don't want to risk our friendship."

"Not going to happen."

"You can't know that." Eric glanced over at Rosie, but she didn't have any advice to offer. "Can we keep things strings-free for now?"

Bridge frowned. "Like friends with benefits?"

He nodded and backed up a foot.

"What if I want more than friends with benefits?" Bridge reached for him, and Eric took another step back.

"It's been a long time since you've been with a man, Bridge, and it was only the once, right? An experiment? You may find it's fun to take the old horse out for another ride but that it's not really the right horse for you . . . or that you want to ride all the horses in the pasture. And if things go bad, I'm out four really good friends."

Bridge pushed his hat back a little with his brush hand, eyebrows furrowing into a scowl. "What are you talking about? I told you last night I didn't suddenly decide I wanted to see what kissing a man was like again. I'm attracted to *you*. Been . . . thinking about you, about kissing *you* for a long time now. I want to go on dates and share my favorite things and learn all your little quirks and turn-ons." Bridge smiled, his voice taking on a wistful note. "Maybe you'll let me be your boyfriend."

"Okay. Slow down, Quick Draw." As much as those words sang like angels in his ears, and it was clear from the look on Bridge's face that he believed what he'd said—for now—Eric couldn't let himself believe in fairy tales again. Not this time. "Let's just . . . keep it on the down low for now, okay?"

"Are you telling me I have to be in the closet when you're not?" Bridge squared his shoulders, adding enough perceived inches to his height to be more than a little intimidating, yet it had the opposite effect on Eric.

"No! Hell no. Just . . ." Eric ran his free hand back and forth over his buzzed head. "Make sure you're certain before you come busting out with all guns blazing. That's all."

Bridge regarded him for a long moment then shrugged, that familiar teasing sparkle returning to his eyes. "Okay. I'll play your way for now, but you'd better start thinking about how you want the crow you're going to be eating prepared when you realize we're going to be more than friends with bennies. You'll see. We're going to be boyfriends."

Eric couldn't help smiling at his friend's confidence, even as a trickle of doubt threaded through his chest. "Sure. Whatever you say."

Bridge grinned, lifting his mug for a quick sip. "Believe me or don't—the result will be the same."

"Believe what?"

Eric startled at the sound of Kent's voice and hated the feeling that he'd been caught with his hands in the cookie jar. Kent led his roping horse to the open space beside Rosie and looped the lead through a ring. Fortunately, Bridge didn't look at all concerned and spoke up without missing a beat, because Eric's voice had flown the coop at that moment.

"Just a little private bet with our good friend here," Bridge said, which was so not the save Eric would have gone for, and then the man had the audacity to wink at him.

"Oh?" Kent looked between the two of them before his gaze settled on Eric, and Eric knew those keen eyes saw more than he wanted them to. "Care to share?"

Eric shook his head, shooting a quick warning glare at Bridge before checking his watch . . . that he'd forgotten to put on. "I gotta go make sure my emergency kit is stocked up." Before either man could make another comment, he turned and hightailed it back to his camper. If the rest of the guys found out he and Bridge were . . . involved, they'd make more out of it than it was, and that was an added pressure Eric knew he wouldn't be able to deal with. They'd expect it to be something more than it was; the kind of expectations that scared the hell out of Eric.

Kent remained quiet until Eric was well out of earshot, but Bridge knew a full-on interrogation was brewing. He began counting down in his head: *five . . . four . . . three . . . two . . .*

"What was that about?"

*. . . one.*

*Damn, he's pulling a Quick Draw McGraw today.*

Bridge rolled a shoulder in a lazy half shrug, put his coffee mug on the trailer's tire well, and returned to grooming Rosie. "Nothing. Just goofing around."

"That's what I'm afraid of." Kent grabbed a brush from the tack box he'd dropped on the ground beside his horse.

"Dude. Really?" Bridge let his gaze follow his hand as he brushed Rosie's sleek coat instead of meeting Kent's eyes. "Kind of all adults here."

Bridge ignored the silence that fell between them and mentally wandered off to replay the conversation with Eric and that last kiss—the perfect meld of those warm, soft lips to his, and the slide of Eric's tongue in his mouth. The enticing taste of him. And, oh God, the feel of the man's hard cock pressing against his thigh seriously had him wanting to follow the natural course of their growing desire. Damn and then some. Just knowing Eric wanted him that much had made his pulse stampede through his body and threatened to disconnect his brain.

"Oh, dude, no." Kent walked around the horses to stand beside him. "You went there, didn't you?"

He wasn't about to lie to Kent by denying it, but he had agreed to keep it on the down low for now. Even so, he couldn't help sliding a glance over his shoulder and wiggling an eyebrow. If he wasn't using words, he wasn't really telling, right? It wasn't his fault if Kent was astute enough to guess on his own.

Kent sighed like a father at the end of his rope with a recalcitrant child. "You'd better not fuck everything up."

"Jeez, dude." Bridge paused his brushing to level a look at Kent that he hoped made clear how much he intended not to fuck everything up. "This isn't just some whim or experiment. I really do like him."

Kent stared back at him, eyes searching, like he could see right into Bridge's brain and read everything in his mind. "Holy hell, you are serious."

Bridge smiled. "Like a bull seeing red."

"Well, I'll be." Kent started to smile, but then it froze partway. "When are you going to tell Marty?"

"When I'm good and ready to." Bridge looked away from Kent and reached into his tack box, trading the brush for a comb and began to tackle Rosie's mane. There really wasn't much to tell yet anyway. Not really. Yeah, he was hot for Eric, and yeah, those kisses had been amazing, but it hadn't been even twenty-four hours yet. Plus, there was the whole keeping-under-the-radar thing . . . that he just blew. "Can't I enjoy this quietly for at least one day?"

"Yeah, but the thing is, you've never been with a man before."

*That's not quite true, actually.* Bridge stopped combing and scowled at his best friend. "Your point, Nosey Parker?"

Kent volleyed with a scowl of his own, but his voice was even when he spoke. "My point is, keeping Marty in the dark isn't right. We don't keep secrets from each other. Especially if they're as big as this."

A sliver of guilt trickled into Bridge's gut at never having seen the point of telling them about his one-time experience. But . . .

"Marty didn't tell us about Tripp for months," Bridge countered, like that would somehow cancel out his omission.

"And," Kent continued, shaking his head as he walked back over to his horse, "considering he's the gay one between us—or was—he's going to be pissed at you for not going straight to him the second you started thinking about Eric as anything more than just a friend."

"I'm sorry. *What?*"

Bridge and Kent both spun around. Marty stood staring at them, wide-eyed and slack-jawed. Heat exploded across Bridge's cheeks. Fuck. Not even seven in the morning and already the day was proving too long. He braced himself for the lashings of yet another earful.

"You're in for it now, buddy," Kent said, slanting a sympathetic half smile his way before turning to Marty. "Mornin', Smarts," Kent added, with a little too much joviality in his voice. He untied his horse while Marty and Bridge stood silent, facing off against each other like a couple of bulls ready to charge, waiting for Kent to leave so they could talk privately.

Marty crossed his arms and pressed his mouth into a flat line. He raised an eyebrow in challenge, waiting for Bridge to start the conversation.

Bridge sighed, took off his hat to run a hand through his hair, and then replaced it. No point in trying to put it off or beating around the bush. "I'm attracted to Eric."

*Riiiip. Off with the Band-Aid!*

Marty continued to stare him down. Not moving, not speaking, but there was definitely a growing anger in his controlled expression.

"And I kissed him." Bridge dropped his eyes for a second, fighting the smile that wanted to break out on his face at the memory. "Twice."

"Are you telling me—" Marty's voice was low, flat, which was a little more nerve-racking than if he'd yelled. Marty mad was a rare thing. "—that you've been gay all this time and never once thought to tell me? Of *all* people?"

"No. I'm not gay." And he immediately regretted the words when an emotion akin to hurt flashed through Marty's green eyes.

"You're attracted to a man," Marty said in that same low voice. "Romantically. That's generally considered being gay."

"But I'm still attracted to women." He dropped the comb into the tack box and then shoved both hands into his pockets. "I just really like Eric."

"So you're bi. Fine." Marty's voice softened, his brief anger fading quickly. "If you get involved with Eric, then you're in a gay relationship."

"Okay, fine. But do we have to label everything so neatly? So he's a guy." Bridge shrugged. "Big deal. I like him. A lot. Isn't that enough?"

Marty studied him for a moment and then sighed, dropping his arms to his sides. "How long?"

Bridge's mouth stretched into a wide smile of its own accord. "Pretty much since the first day we met him, back at the hospital in Santa Maria last spring."

"I meant, how long have you known you're attracted to men, too? People don't generally wake up in their late twenties and suddenly decide they're bisexual or gay."

"Oh." Bridge looked down at his boots, chewed at his lower lip, and then met Marty's gaze. "I, uh, kind of fooled around with a guy in college. Once."

The look Marty leveled at him went straight to his gut like a knife. He'd never once thought not telling about that time would come back around and end up hurting one of the very best friends he'd ever had.

"I'm sorry, Marty," Bridge said. "It's not that I didn't want to tell you or that I was hiding anything. It's just . . . Remember Silvie?" He waited until Marty nodded before continuing. "Well, I met her right after, and I figured since she turned me on so much so fast that the thing with that guy was just one of those college experience things. You know how that goes."

"Not really," Marty said. The hurt Bridge had seen in his eyes dissipated, thankfully, leaving behind only understanding. Then Marty smiled. "That explains a lot, I guess."

"What do you mean?"

"I'm not really all that shocked you'd find yourself interested in a man. I mean, you've never had any issues at all with showing affection for us, kissing our cheeks and hugging and stuff, or pointing out hot guys for me. Then I noticed those odd looks you had on your face when Eric was around. I kind of thought something was up and wanted to ask, but there was too much going on with Tripp at the time."

Bridge smiled, relief flooding into his veins. "So, you're not mad at me?"

"Of course I'm mad at you! You should have told me."

"I'm sorry, Smarts. I was going to, but the timing was bad for a while there and I wasn't even really sure what was going on. I didn't want to add more crap to your pile. It wasn't until last night that I finally geared myself up enough to talk to Eric about it. And then we kissed, and well, it's kind of all I can think about right now . . ."

The corners of Marty's mouth lifted, and his eyes glittered. "So it was good then?"

Bridge moaned his delight. "Best. Ever."

"I should have known." Marty shook his head and chuckled. "You stuck by me like it was nothing when I came out."

"Well, duh," Bridge said. "We're practically brothers."

"Even brothers still turn away sometimes," Marty said, a note of sadness in his voice.

"They're just assholes then, aren't they?"

He met Marty's gaze and opened his arms. Marty stepped into the embrace and wrapped around him.

"I'm happy for you. I really am. *But* . . ." Marty disengaged, stepping back to level a warning glare on him. "I know you wouldn't mess around with Eric unless you're dead serious about him, so make sure this is what you want. Okay? I'd hate to see him get his heart broken."

Bridge threw his arms up, exasperated, and looked to the sky for help. "Why does everyone think *I'm* going to break *his* heart?"

# CHAPTER
## SEVEN

"**D**ude. Stop already."

Bridge jerked at the sound of Marty's voice and turned to see three sets of eyes on him. Marty looking annoyed, Tripp amused, and Cory somewhere between entertained and lost. "What?"

"The knee thing." Marty motioned with a flip of his hand. "It's getting old."

"Oh." Bridge stopped bouncing his knee and took a long draught of his beer. "Sorry."

He hadn't realized he'd been doing it, but shit, how long were those guys going to keep playing poker? A man's patience could only stretch so far. He'd opted out of playing because he didn't have the money he knew he'd lose given all his attention would be on Eric rather than the game. That and Cory had come by again to talk shop. Now Bridge just wanted everyone to leave so he could get Eric alone. Right fucking now. Before he burst his damn seams.

Tripp clapped him on the shoulder. "Don't worry, man. The game's almost over."

"Shut up," Bridge grumbled, and glared at Marty.

"What? Like I'm not going to tell Tripp?"

"Tell Tripp what?" Cory asked, leaning forward, his eyes bright with anticipation of juicy gossip.

"Nothing, kid," Bridge said.

Cory sat up straight and threw his shoulders back. "I am not a kid. I'll have you know I turned twenty-two just last month."

Bridge couldn't help the laughter that bubbled up at the indignant tone in Cory's voice, and when Marty and Tripp joined in, it drew the attention of the card players fifteen feet away. But it was Eric's gaze locking on his that made his skin burn and ache for the man's touch.

All damn day he could think of nothing but Eric and the feel of him in his arms and kissing him and all the things he wanted to do to him, with him. Fortunately, he'd had a lot of work to provide much-needed reprieves, but when they were between demonstrations and waiting for chutes to open, his brain was completely overrun by one smoking-hot ex–New Yorker.

But tradition wouldn't be forsaken, and for the last hour-plus, he'd sat there with Marty, Tripp, and Cory, talking everything rodeo and pickup riding and praying for that damn game to come to an end. All the while, his impatience continued its ascent into the unbearable.

Finally the last hand was tossed, and after a round of good-natured jibes and laughs, Kent leaned over to scoop up his winnings.

Bridge released a long sigh of relief and whispered, "Thank Christ."

He stood and said his good-byes to Cory and Toby, both of whom he likely wouldn't see again after the clinic ended tomorrow, and to Craig and Rowdy, with promises to join the table when rodeo season officially started in a couple of weeks.

Then it was him and his four friends, standing at equal intervals around the dying campfire between their trailers, and for some reason, Bridge thought it should mean something profound, like each of them possessed a quality that required the combination of all five to ignite it, like doing so formed a balance or some sort of force that could never be broken.

Like a five-point star with Eric at the top, at least to him. He knew his friends were all around him, but at the moment, the only one he could see was Eric, standing there with his hands in his pockets and a tease of a smile on his handsome face. The top point of his star.

*Oh my God. I'm turning into a total sap.* Funny how it didn't seem to bother him, though. He'd happily be a sap for Eric any day. He huffed a soft chuckle, earning curious looks from the guys. They could keep on being curious because he sure as hell wasn't going to share his thoughts just then.

"And on that note," Marty said with laughter in his voice. He smacked Eric playfully on the shoulder as he and Tripp turned for their RV. "Play safe, boys."

Kent chuckled. "Shall I leave the light on?"

Bridge groaned and shook his head, turning away to avoid making eye contact with Eric. "You guys are such dicks," he said under his breath, but a note of amusement still rang through his voice.

"Yeah, that's why you love us," Kent said, and turned to open the door to their rig. "Don't forget to make sure the fire's out before you pack it in."

"Yes, boss," Bridge said, laughing when Kent flipped him off without looking back.

The second the door closed and they were alone, Eric rounded on him. "What part of down low didn't you understand?"

"Dude." Bridge raised his hands in surrender. Yes, he felt bad that he'd let the cat out of the bag already and knew he'd get an earful for it, but at the same time, he was glad he didn't have to try to keep how he was feeling in check. Eric pushed too many of his buttons for him not to slip up at an inopportune time. "They kind of already guessed, and besides, it's just the guys. You know they're all cool with us getting together."

Eric raised an eyebrow, not seeming appeased. "There are going to be expectations now. They'll think we're more than we are."

Bridge frowned, not liking the way those words grated on him. "Why don't you want them to know?"

"It's not that." Eric ran a hand over his head, the movement choppy, agitated. "Did we not agree, just this morning, that there'd be no strings? *And* keep it quiet until—*if*—you're sure you want to come out? They're going to treat us like a couple now, and we aren't."

*But we will be.* Bridge bit back the words and the sharp stab of disappointment in his chest at Eric's hesitation. "I really don't see that being a problem, and I'm getting a little tired of everyone telling me to make sure I'm sure. The second I saw you the other day, I was certain." Bridge dipped his head to look closer into Eric's eyes and once again saw that flicker of fear and trepidation in their depths. Whatever had happened in Eric's past to put that there, he wanted to find a way to chase it off for good. They could be so much more together; he knew that right down to the bottom of his gut. But that would only happen if Eric gave them a chance. "I'm sorry. I really didn't mean to say anything, but Kent kind of guessed and Marty overheard, so . . ."

Eric shook his head, releasing a sigh that sounded somewhere between resignation and relief. "All guns blazing. Only way you can do anything, isn't it?"

"That's how I ride, baby," he teased, hoping a little levity would push the clouds from Eric's eyes. He took a step closer. "Forgive me?"

"You're going to be the end of me," Eric finally said, but he smiled, that lone dimple making a welcome appearance.

"As long as you go with a smile on your face." Bridge stepped right into Eric's space and gripped him by the hips, pulling him in so their bodies were flush against each other. When Eric's arms snaked around his waist and tightened, Bridge's whole body sighed. *Yes.* This was what he needed. Just being able to touch Eric, to feel his heat, to smell his cologne and that trace of sweat . . . That was all it took to make the world align in a sense of complete rightness. Eric did that.

"I just need you to slow down, okay?"

Bridge couldn't do more than nod in response. He leaned down and nuzzled his nose into Eric's neck and breathed deeply. God, that was becoming one of his favorite things. He shivered when Eric's tongue, hot and wet, traced the curve of his earlobe and then dipped inside, drawing a soft moan up from the bottom of Bridge's throat.

"Oh. That's a spot, is it?" Eric's moist breath sent a tremor rumbling through his whole body, pinging through his veins and heightening his every sense.

And it was fucking hot.

He tried to say so, but the words got all jumbled and couldn't break free. Whatever noise of agreement he managed to make seemed to be enough, though, because Eric went at his ear again, and holy shit . . . Had he ever been this turned on before?

Bridge slid his hand down Eric's arm, slipped it into Eric's, and laced their fingers. He leaned into Eric's ear and ran his tongue along the shell, just the way Eric had done to him, and smiled at the tremble he drew from the man. He whispered, "I really think you should take me to your camper now."

Eric leaned back and looked at him, a mixture of anticipation and apprehension seeping back into his expression.

Nope that wouldn't do. "You look a little worried."

"You sure this is what you want?"

Bridge rocked his hips forward, letting Eric feel just how sure he was. "All guns ablaze."

Hesitation seeped from Eric's violet depths, and they darkened, flecks of silver flashed, and his voice was a low rumble when he spoke. "Put out the fire."

Not letting go of Eric's hand, he kicked dirt into the small pit until any still-glowing embers had been extinguished. "Let's go." The urgency in his voice matched the urgency of his steps as they walked the short distance and stumbled into Eric's camper like a couple of hormonal teenagers.

Bridge froze just inside the doorway, staring at the small space while Eric squeezed in behind him and locked the door. There was almost no room for one grown man, let alone two. On one side of a narrow hall was a micro kitchen, on the other side, a bench seat running the length of the camper and a tiny table. But more importantly . . . "Where the hell's the bed?"

Eric pointed to a cubbyhole-sized space at the front of the camper above the cab of the truck. It couldn't have been more than three feet high.

There was no way. "Are you serious? We won't both fit up there."

"Don't worry," Eric said, wrapping his arms around Bridge's waist from behind, palms flat on his stomach, and kissed his ear. "The table drops down to make a bigger bed."

"Mmm, good." He let his head fall back onto Eric's shoulder, and his hat fell to the floor. So long as Eric kept doing that, nothing else really mattered. And it wasn't like he'd never made out in the backseat of a car before, so this was a step up. "That feels so good."

"Yeah?" Eric kissed the side of his neck and gently sucked the skin there, teasing it with his tongue. "How about that?"

"Yes. More." He turned in Eric's arms and lowered his head to claim Eric's mouth. All day he'd been replaying the last kiss they'd shared. All day he'd been dreaming of kissing this man again. And now, finally, he got his wish, and somehow it was even better than the last time. They fit perfectly. Their noses didn't bump because he seemed to instinctively know which way to angle his head, and Eric seemed to know how to tease and caress his tongue, how much to give and take, how to deepen the kiss to the point where Bridge felt like his whole body was melting into Eric's.

He pulled back just enough to swallow a gulp of air. "Fuck, Eric." Their lips brushed as he spoke, his voice a rasp. "No one has ever turned me on like you do. It's like all the wires in my brain short-circuit."

Eric leaned back a little and ducked his head, a slight blush coloring his cheeks. "I bet you say that to all the cowboys."

"You're not a cowboy." Bridge raised a hand and ran it over Eric's head, like he'd been wanting to for days now. The close-cropped hair under his palm was fuzzy, softer than he'd expected. "You don't even have a proper hat."

Eric leaned into Bridge's gentle massage and sighed. "I'll get one. Tomorrow."

"You barely know how to ride a horse."

"Ah, but I know how to ride you." Eric's accent had thickened, his voice lower.

Bridge stared down at Eric, who looked up through a fan of dark eyelashes. Simple words, but the images they conjured in his mind had his synapses snapping like popcorn. *Danger, danger, Will Robinson.* "Yes. God, yes."

Eric graced him with a sly, seductive smile. "We'll get there. We have lots of options to explore."

"Then let's get exploring!" There was that childhood Christmas-morning feeling again, when Bridge had been so excited, he couldn't decide where to start, so he just dove in headfirst.

Which is what he tried to do with Eric's clothing now. Trembling, he pushed Eric's jacket out of the way and began unbuttoning his shirt with one hand while tugging at his belt buckle with the other. He needed more hands. Eric laughed, the sound like music to his ears.

"Easy there, Quick Draw." Eric placed his hands over Bridge's to slow him down. "First, I'm going to give you the best blowjob of your life."

Bridge stopped. So did his breath. And maybe his heart, too. Then a deep, chest-rumbling groan rattled up his throat. "Yes, yes, yes. Please, yes."

Eric guided Bridge's hands to his sides and then let go and spun them around so Bridge's back was to the door. "Stay," he said, smirking when Bridge scowled at him, and turned to walk the few feet to the end of the sitting area.

"Really?" Bridge put his hands on his hips but had to drop them when his elbow banged into the tiny fridge. He rubbed at it absently. "You're going to fire me up like that and then walk away?"

Eric only slanted a crooked smile over his shoulder, leaning down to release a latch under the little table. He lowered it until it was level with the bench, pulled the cushions down and placed them on top of the table, and then yanked the sheets off the bed up top and haphazardly spread them out over the cushions.

He turned back to Bridge with that big dimpled grin in place and spread his arm over the table-bed in invitation. "This might be a little more comfortable than standing in that narrow entryway, don't you think?"

Bridge barely took two full strides before he was once again plastered against Eric's lithe body, his momentum tipping Eric over and sending them both crashing onto the makeshift bed in a tangle of legs and arms. It creaked a loud complaint, and Bridge braced himself for the give, but it held their weight. The bed was just wide enough for the two of them, if they didn't mind spooning, but it was too short for him to stretch out to his full height. His feet dangled off the side, and he chuckled. "This Tonka truck of yours is too small. We're definitely going to need a bigger bed."

Something dark passed through Eric's eyes too fast for Bridge to decipher, but he forgot all about trying to figure it out when Eric pushed at his shoulders, rolling him over and straddling his hips in one swift move. The shock of being so easily manhandled charged him in a way he'd never thought possible, quickening his pulse, stealing his breath, and making a newfound need for more roar in his head. That was . . . unexpected, exciting, enticing. Then Eric's weight settled on him, butt nestling against Bridge's rapidly swelling cock, and another wave of need tore through him. Eric rocked a little and then leaned forward, dropping to support himself on arms that bracketed Bridge's head, and instead of the kiss he'd expected, Eric ran his tongue along the groove of Bridge's chin.

"I've wanted to do that longer than I care to admit," Eric said, and then followed the confession with a kiss before Bridge could speak. But who really cared about words just then, because when Eric rolled his hips forward, hard erection pressing into Bridge's navel, he couldn't remember ever feeling anything so amazing.

And they were both still fully clothed.

Which brought to mind his interrupted mission of unwrapping Eric like a Christmas present. "Clothes." He pushed Eric's jacket off his shoulders, but it got caught at the man's wrists, earning a grunt of frustration from Bridge. "They gotta go. All of 'em."

"We've got all night, cowboy." Eric chuckled and sat up, stripped himself of the jacket, and tossed it on the floor.

"And we best get to making the most of it," Bridge said. He didn't know if there would be another night after this, if Eric would wake up in the morning and decide screwing with their friendship really was a bad idea. That wasn't going to happen if he could help it, though. He couldn't predict the future, but right now, this very moment, he knew he wouldn't accept anything less than a life with Eric Palmer.

Eric smiled and began unbuttoning his shirt, but Bridge reached out and stilled his hands. "Let me," he said, his voice a breathy whisper.

Bridge watched his fingers as they worked, feeling the weight of Eric's stare on him, the press of Eric's body in his lap, the burning caress of Eric's hands where they rested on his torso, and a thrill of excitement trembled through him. Eric leaned down and kissed his forehead, above his brow, his nose.

Fuck, he couldn't ever remember feeling this high, this alive, or so completely aroused. Not with the one man he'd been with before, not with any of the women he'd been with, but Eric . . . Eric was in a whole other zip code of desire and want. He was like Christmas, Easter, Thanksgiving, and a birthday all in one. Better even. Yes, definitely better. By far.

Not because anyone before had been bad or lacking, but the fact that it was Eric made every contact and look somehow . . . more.

He slipped the last button through its hole and then slowly parted Eric's shirt to reveal a lightly furred chest, defined abs, and honey-colored skin that looked like it might taste just as sweet. His mouth watered at the sight, and he licked his lips.

"Touch me," Eric whispered.

Bridge looked up to meet Eric's eyes. They were dark, glittering, devouring him without even touching him, and fuck, he couldn't stop trembling. He flattened his hands over soft skin and hard pectorals and slid upward, nudging the shirt off Eric's shoulders, following it down impressive biceps until the shirt caught at bent elbows, but Eric didn't move. He sat still, watching, letting Bridge explore at will.

He brought his hands back to Eric's stomach, let his fingers ride the small roller coaster rise and fall of firm muscle and solid rib, and then circled dusky, peaked nipples. He rolled them between his forefingers and thumbs, and a groan spilled from Eric, and his eyelids fluttered; Bridge couldn't help the smile that stretched across his face. "Found a spot, did I?"

Eric chuckled. "Just you wait." He slid his arms the rest of the way out of his shirt, and with the most seductive grin Bridge had ever been on the receiving end of, Eric said, "My turn."

Eric reached out and began working the buttons of Bridge's shirt, and Bridge let his hands slide over the heated skin of Eric's sides to grip the dense muscles of his back, marveling at the feel of so much power under his palms, wanting to experience the full force of that power, to know what it would be like to have it unleashed on him.

And then skillful hands were on his skin, palms flat, moving over the surface of his chest, his abs, his navel, and their heat sent his skin ablaze, leaving an inferno in their wake that melted his bones. His breath came faster, shallow and raspy, and his heart pounded a rapid beat against his rib cage. And they still had their damn pants on. He was about to make his dismay known when the hot cavern of Eric's mouth covered one of his nipples, and *pop*, there went all his mental capacity. Sharp jolts of electricity blasted outward, inward, everywhere, and he arched into the kiss, the bite. Whatever, just so long as Eric didn't stop. "Holy Jesus!"

No one ever had done that to him before. If he'd known what a sensitive erotic spot it was, he'd have begged for it every chance he got. And now that he knew, he'd beg Eric for it, shamelessly and often.

Eric lifted himself and slanted another knock-you-on-your-ass flirtatious grin at him. "We haven't even started, cowboy."

"Oh good God." Bridge rocked his hips in search of friction, release from the confines of his jeans, anything to get closer, faster. "I'm not going to survive."

Eric laughed and pinched the sensitive nipple he'd been sucking on, sending another shock straight into Bridge's groin, like the two were somehow connected. "I think you will, and you'll beg for more."

Bridge moaned, dug his fingers into the flesh of Eric's back, and stared up into those captivating violet eyes, casting a plea with his own. "I'm begging right now."

"What do you want?"

"Fuck, I love your accent," Bridge said, voice reedy.

The light in Eric's eyes flickered again, but then there was nothing in them aside from lust and desire. That seductive grin grew wider, topped off by a voice dripping in sex. "What do you want?"

Bridge panted like a damned dog, but he couldn't care less. All he wanted was whatever Eric was willing to give him. "More."

"More what?"

"More everything! Just don't stop."

Bridge made to sit up, take over, but Eric held him down with a hand planted in the middle of his chest, and again, his breath caught with that unexpected thrill of a simple display of power. All the women he'd dated over the years had been athletic, strong—physically and mentally—and could throw down with the best of them, but not one had ever used that in bed. He didn't know if it was the new power dynamic Eric introduced, or Eric himself, but now that Bridge had gotten a little taste, he knew he wanted more.

Eric cocked his head slightly, grinning, like he knew what Bridge was thinking. He leaned down and peppered his lips with quick, playful kisses, until Bridge opened his mouth and Eric dove in. Jesus, the way the man kissed, like he wanted everything, couldn't get enough, demanding as much as he gave. Bridge liked kissing—a lot—but he couldn't put his finger on why kissing Eric was so much different. He'd never actually kissed the guy he'd fooled around with in college, so Eric was his first, but that wasn't it. There was something more there, something deeper that made every kiss he'd experienced before pale in comparison. Maybe it was the way they fit or how incredible Eric tasted. More likely it was Eric. Whatever it was, it was rapidly becoming his new favorite thing.

Eric broke the kiss, leaving Bridge gasping, and moved down Bridge's body, kissing and licking a burning trail down his torso, Eric's talented tongue circling around his belly button and dipping inside while agile hands deftly popped the buttons of his jeans. *Yes, yes, yes.* One of those hot, callused hands slipped beneath the layers of denim and cotton and cupped his balls, pressed against the base of his cock, and slowly, maddeningly followed the length to its tip. Then Eric mouthed him through his underwear, and he damn near jolted right off the bed—he'd thought the shock of his nipples being sucked was electric? *Holy shit and damn.* There were no words for this, and there was still that thin barrier of cotton between them.

Eric tugged at the waist of his jeans. "Up." One word but his voice cracked and sounded like it had been dragged over sharp gravel.

Bridge reacted without thought, immediately lifting his hips so Eric could pull his jeans and boxers off. They got caught on his boots, but Eric didn't bother to remove them, just left him shackled around the ankles and crawled back up Bridge's body. A wicked grin and a waggle of eyebrows was the only warning he got before Eric dipped down, swallowing Bridge's cock in one smooth motion. The head nudged the back of Eric's throat when Eric's nose disappeared in the thatch of light-brown pubic hair at the base of Bridge's dick, and a sharp chin pressed against his balls.

"Holy . . . mother . . ." His vocabulary vanished. His eyes tried to roll into the back of his head, but he fought them with everything he had. He did not want to miss a single second of watching Eric go down on him. He wanted to brand every second of it into his memory permanently. Forever. Until the end of time and then some, for good measure.

Eric slid to the tip, his cheeks hollowing as he suctioned his way up. He rolled his tongue around the head and dipped into the slit, and Bridge didn't think he could last a second longer even as he struggled to last as long as possible. His eyes squeezed shut against his control, and his head fell back. He may have shouted something. He didn't know. Didn't care. He just didn't want Eric to stop whatever he was doing, but at the same time, his balls where beginning to fill and tighten, and he knew he was rapidly approaching the point of no return.

"So. Fucking. Close," he panted.

Eric bobbed on his dick and the camper shook and clothing rustled and the teeth of a zipper echoed in the small space. Bridge snapped his eyes open, looked down, and saw Eric take himself in hand and begin to stroke in time to his bobbing.

"Don't come yet," Bridge said, breathless.

Eric looked up at him and fuck, how many times was he going to discover something hotter than the last thing he'd thought was the hottest thing he'd ever seen? But this, Eric staring at him with those intense, glittering violet eyes, pink lips stretched around his dick, a hand wrapped around his own as he jacked himself . . . Bridge added that image to the permanent archives in his mental museum.

"I wanna see you come."

Eric smiled around the column of flesh in his mouth, lowered his eyes, and let go of his erection to wrap his hand around the base of Bridge's cock. With invigorated determination, he worked Bridge until his entire world narrowed to the point where they met, Eric's mouth and hand around his cock—firm, tantalizing, perfect. That was the whole universe. He didn't need anything else. Not a single thing. Not oxygen, not water. Only Eric and his magic hands and mouth and tongue. The orgasm exploded so suddenly, with so much force, it shattered even the tiniest shred of lingering doubt in his mind that this could ever be just friends with benefits. This was it. Eric was it. He knew it like he knew he needed to breathe. He shouted out his ecstasy with such sheer abandon that he thought for sure the entire rodeo grounds would hear.

When he was finally able to piece two coherent thoughts together, he opened his eyes to see Eric kneeling above him: his hand a blur as it flew up and down his cock, his chest and neck flushed, and his mouth open. Completely lost in his own impending orgasm. And then he groaned and grunted and jerked thick ropes of cum onto Bridge's stomach. Hot whips of liquid hit his skin.

Eric's stroking slowed, and his chest rose and fell in rapid succession, his breathing harsh and shallow. He looked down at Bridge, a lazy, sated smile on his swollen, red lips.

"That was by far the hottest fucking thing I have ever seen," Bridge said, still marveling at the beauty of it.

Eric dragged his fingers through the sticky mess, making little circles and figure eights in it, then brought his fingers to his mouth and sucked them inside.

Bridge's breath caught, and his heart skipped a beat. "Oh God. I take it back. *That's* the hottest thing by far. Ever."

Eric smiled, a hint of mischievousness in the curve of his mouth, and he repeated the slow drag through the cooling puddle. But this time, he brought his fingers to Bridge's mouth. Bridge opened, sucked them inside, and the flavor of Eric—sharp, bitter but somehow sweet, too—blasted over his tongue, and he groaned, closing his eyes. Best taste in the world.

"Now that," Eric said, his accent more pronounced, "is fucking hot." He traced Bridge's lower lip, gaze following his finger, and then he looked up and winked. "By far."

Bridge slid a hand around the back of Eric's neck and pulled him down for a kiss. It was slow and sensual and content and just fucking perfect in every way. Eric lowered himself until he was flush against Bridge, and the burning heat of skin on skin eased Bridge in a way he never thought was possible. The kiss was too good to interrupt for something as mundane as cleaning up or taking off the rest of their clothes.

But Eric pulled back and smiled. "As much as I could fall asleep right now, I think we'd be more comfortable not shackled by our pants and half-hanging off the side of the bed."

Bridge sighed, feigning annoyance. "So high maintenance."

A few moments later, they were stretched out under the covers, Bridge's arm wrapped around Eric's shoulders, Eric's head on his chest and an arm draped across his stomach.

"You're right," Bridge said.

"About?"

"That was the best blowjob of my life. By far."

Eric laughed, and the sound, soft and soothing, sent Bridge into peaceful slumber with a smile on his face.

Eric woke to the sound of merrily chirping birds, a sated happiness he wasn't sure he'd ever felt, and a big, warm body wrapped around him like a blanket. The smile that spread across his face did so without any effort on his part. He opened his eyes. Their foreheads were close enough for Bridge's bangs to tickle his brow, but the hair was soft, and he didn't want to move a single muscle for fear of disturbing the moment. Long, sooty lashes formed crescents on high cheekbones. Bridge's lips were parted slightly, a touch swollen from the frenetic kissing the night before, and there was a hint of whisker burn on his chin. He didn't seem to have as much facial hair, or hair elsewhere, as Eric did. He lowered his gaze. Bridge's chest was smooth, save for a few golden hairs that gathered in a sunny swirl around his rose-colored nipples. Faint freckles scattered over otherwise unblemished pale skin, and Eric's mouth watered with the desire to lick every inch of him.

He couldn't see any more of the man without disturbing him. Both of the stalwart cowboy's arms were wrapped around him, holding him close. One muscular leg was draped over his hip and hooked behind his thigh. His leg was tucked between Bridge's legs, his knee high enough that he could just feel the tickle of fine hairs on Bridge's heavy balls at the apex of those long legs.

Hard silken skin nudged at his groin, drawing an answering throb from his cock as it began to rise, but he held himself still. Bridge had to set the pace for their sexual explorations—if there would even be more after last night. Part of him wanted Bridge to wake up and say, *Well, that was fun but maybe this wasn't such a good idea after all.* Things would be easier that way. Then Eric could relax back into the easy friendship he'd found with this tight band of cowboys, and Bridge would never have an opportunity to discover whatever was inside Eric that made him unworthy of truly belonging. But another part of him, the part that longed for something he'd given up on, needed more of the way Bridge had looked at him last night—with so much open abandon and trust and desire—and craved the power to make Bridge squirm and his breath catch and his body tremble in pleasure. That had been heady, dangerous, and was the stuff that would get him in big trouble if he didn't keep things in perspective. If he let his guard down, he'd fall hard and fast. He knew he'd never be able to recover from Bridge walking away from him like everyone else had.

*But this time might be different.*

He quickly shot that hopeful little voice down. It never won.

He lifted his gaze to find an open pair of warm, comforting eyes staring at him intently. No panic at what they'd done lurked in the depths, no regret. Just a naked hunger that made his heart beat faster while sending a little trickle of fear snaking into his veins.

A teasing smile tipped up the edges of Bridge's mouth, and he rolled his hips, pressing a now rock-hard erection against Eric's. Then Bridge leaned forward and kissed him, slow and lazy and familiar, like they'd been waking up side by side for years instead of for the first time. The kind of kiss Eric had dreamed of but had not dared hope for. Now that he'd had a taste, he didn't know if he could keep things as detached as he needed in order to protect himself, but he did know going back to the way things were before last night wasn't ever going to happen.

Bridge pulled back and kissed the tip of Eric's nose. "What do you say we start the day right?" His voice was deeper than usual and rough with sleep.

Eric stared into that eager, handsome face and knew there was no way he could say no, just as he knew Bridge would soon realize Eric wasn't what he really wanted and move on. If Eric kept that in the front of his mind, then he could enjoy this gift for what it was.

Eric buried the chatter in his head and smiled. "Good call, I say." He slid a hand between them, closed it around both of their cocks, and stroked them as one. Slow, firm, gently squeezing the heads together.

"Fuck, that feels good." Bridge's eyelids fluttered, but his gaze remained locked on Eric's, and the hand resting on Eric's hip tightened.

"Mm-hmm."

Bridge rocked into his grip, and Eric marveled at how well they fit together, how frighteningly comfortable being here like this felt. He increased the speed of his strokes, and Bridge thrust harder. Hot breath gusted over his cheek in fast, harsh pants, and he knew this wasn't going to be a leisurely ride but a balls-out race to the finish line. His own breath scraped and clawed its way out, and the groans and growls that lingered in the back of his throat were echoed by the man whose dark eyes he could not pull away from.

"Come with," Bridge whispered, and then a large hand closed over Eric's and together the beat sped up as they both charged for the exit gate, exploding out into the wild as one. Bridge's mouth fell open in a silent yell, and Eric pressed his forehead to Bridge's, finally forcing that long, intense stare into submission.

Eric slipped his hand out from under Bridge's and rolled his hips back, needing a little space for his now overly sensitive skin. Bridge kissed him and then flopped onto his back, a satisfied smile gracing his face, and Eric couldn't look away.

Bridge turned his head, and a mischievous glint sparkled in his eyes. Before Eric could question what the man was up to, or get out of striking range, Bridge wiped his hand on Eric's navel, spreading cool, sticky cum onto his skin.

"Hey!" Eric slapped the offending hand away as hearty laughter danced around him. He fought not to laugh, but it was a losing battle. "Ass," he teased.

"Good thing we don't have to sleep here again tonight," Bridge said, the light in his eyes mesmerizing. "You've made a helluva mess of these sheets."

"Me?" Eric huffed, keeping his tone playful even as his mind latched onto the *we* and began a little panic dance in the background. *Sex, Eric*, he scolded himself. *Just sex.*

Bridge watched him for a long moment while their breathing evened out, quieted, and Eric could finally hear the stirrings of life beyond the camper. The affable cowboy's impish expression shifted to something more serious, and a sense of foreboding kicked up the panic dance a notch. Eric didn't even want to guess what was coming, but he had a feeling he wasn't going to like it.

Bridge rolled to his side and rested his head on a hand, reaching out to caress Eric's shoulder with the other. "Did you close up your house for the season yet?"

Eric frowned. Well, that was out of left field. "Uh, no. I was going to head back after the clinic wrapped today."

"Do you have much to do?" Bridge glanced away briefly.

"No, not really. Forward the mail, pack some stuff, leave a key with the neighbors."

"And work? Are you back to on call now?"

Eric nodded, trying to get a grip on his increasing heart rate.

Bridge inhaled a deep breath, like he was shoring up courage, which only increased Eric's apprehension as to where this was headed.

"So . . . I was thinking: why don't you stay here? In Folsom. Come out to the ranch until the season starts and—"

Eric gasped. He didn't mean to, but hell. What was Bridge saying? Move in? After one night and the most amazing blowjob and handjob ever? No. No way. That was not the no-strings, go-slow plan they'd agreed on yesterday.

"I mean, it's only two weeks, right?" Bridge continued in a rush, his voice sounding more urgent, more unsure. "And we're way closer here to the season opener than you. Red Bluff is the weekend after, in your neck of the woods, so you could close up your house then. It would save you all that driving back and forth. That's, like, six hours round-trip, right?" Bridge paused, his gaze imploring, hopeful. "And while you're here, I can give you some more riding lessons, maybe teach you how to rope. Make a real cowboy out of you."

"I . . . uh . . ." *Can't. But I want to.* He ran a hand over his head, stopping to hold the back of his skull in case his conflicted brains decided to spill out. It would be too much time too close to Bridge, which would make it too easy to lose his perspective and fall in too deep.

"I mean . . ." Bridge shrugged and shifted his gaze to follow his hand as it slid a hot path from Eric's shoulder to his elbow and back. "It's not like I'm asking you to move in or anything. We do have two guest rooms, so you'd have your own space. But you know—" Bridge shot him a quick, shy glance, but there was a heat behind it, like the looks Bridge had given him last night, all weekend, and he knew then, good or bad, he was going to give in. "Think of all the sex we could have—and in a real bed that's actually big enough for full-grown men."

Okay. No-strings sex. That was what they'd agreed on, and it would only be two weeks. And he'd have his own room . . . Jesus, he was really considering this.

"What about Kent?"

"No threesomes." Bridge's mouth lifted in a crooked smile.

"You know what I mean, Bridge." His tone was a little harder than he'd intended, but this wasn't a game to him. He knew the risk he was running here and needed some assurance from Bridge that he realized it too, and would respect his boundaries. "We're not dating. We're not boyfriends. We're friends who have sex sometimes. Okay?"

Eric was almost sad to see that teasing smile slip from Bridge's face, but his eyes and voice were sincere when he spoke. "I'll talk to him. Make sure he understands we're just . . . hanging out."

Eric nodded. "Thank you."

"So . . . what do you say, stud?"

Eric studied Bridge for a long moment, taking in the deep-brown eyes with flecks of sunshine in them, how warm and comfortable and safe looking into them made him feel. Fuck. He was so screwed. He knew it. This was not going to end well, but he was so starved for what Bridge was offering, he couldn't find it in him to walk away just yet. He reached out and traced Bridge's lips with a fingertip. "All guns blazing."

Bridge smiled, and his fate was sealed.

# CHAPTER
## EIGHT

Three days and several blowjobs later, Bridge yanked the front door open before Eric's blue Tundra had come to a complete stop in the driveway. He walked to the edge of the front patio barefoot and bounced on his toes, his smile so big, it could split his face in half. Which was silly, considering only ten hours had passed since Eric had been called in to cover a shift in Modesto today. Not even a full twenty-four hours had gone by, yet it felt like it had been a month. He knew Eric was only at work, that he'd return when he was done, but even so, Bridge had found it almost impossible to concentrate all day. Just knowing Eric had been there, that he could look up from whatever he was doing and catch a glimpse, a smile, a flash of that gorgeous dimple, steal a kiss . . . had somehow become important to him.

Eric waved as he parked and killed the engine, and Bridge's mouth watered when Eric sauntered around the side of the vehicle toward him, still wearing his work clothes—dark-blue trousers and a crisp white shirt under a dark-blue jacket with more pockets than Bridge could count. A patch on the jacket bore a paramedic emblem, and underneath it, Eric's name was written in matching blue cursive.

A man in uniform. He could definitely see the appeal now.

"Hey, stud," Bridge said and opened his arms to welcome him home.

"Hey, cowboy." Eric stepped right into the embrace, kissing him like he'd just returned from a week in the desert without water. To which Bridge could relate, because that was exactly how he felt. All day, he'd been trying to quench a thirst that could only be slaked by the hot-as-sin New Yorker currently in his arms. It was then that he not only realized how natural, how right, it had felt to welcome Eric home like this, but that Eric hadn't hesitated. As far as signs went, it was small, but Bridge hoped that maybe Eric was beginning to see how much more they could be, too.

Bridge walked them backward into the house, breaking the kiss only because he stumbled over the weather stripping in the doorway. "I want you so damn bad right now."

"Likewise," Eric said, kicking the door closed with the heel of his shoe.

He pushed Eric up against the door and claimed his mouth in another thirst-quenching kiss. He started plucking at Eric's shirt buttons, urgency rising inside him like a tidal wave.

"Whoa." Eric pulled back, lightly wrapping his hands around Bridge's wrists. "Not here. I doubt Kent wants to see this kind of show."

Bridge slipped out from under those warm hands he knew could do amazing things to his body and returned to his mission: stripping Eric and having his way with him. "I gave him twenty bucks and kicked him out. Told him to quit being a chickenshit and take Lily out for dinner."

Eric laughed and hooked his index fingers in the front pockets of Bridge's jeans, tugging him closer so their groins were flush together. Being so close made it harder for Bridge to undo the lower shirt buttons and slowed him down, but oh, the sweet pressure on his dick was so worth it.

"Marty's sister?" Eric's voice sounded a little breathy, but his accent had sharpened. He kissed Bridge on his neck, just below his ear, and Bridge shivered. "About time, I guess. Never saw that man blush or stumble over his words like he does in her presence."

"Yeah, he's been half in love with her forever, but"—another shiver rattled through him when Eric mouthed his earlobe, tugging it with velvety lips—"he figures she wouldn't be interested in one of his brother's 'annoying' roughneck friends."

He pushed Eric's shirt out of the way and went straight for one of those tight, exposed nipples, circling it with his tongue, sucking it into his mouth. The gasp that escaped Eric made him smile around the pebbled nub.

"And I thought he was the—Jesus, Bridge—smart one of the b-bunch." Eric moved his hands to cup Bridge's ass and pulled them tighter together, increasing the friction on his straining erection.

"I love that I just made you stutter," Bridge whispered and moved to the other nipple, a swell of joy spreading throughout this chest. He did that to the sexy paramedic. Being able to give that to him, knowing he could, filled Bridge with a sense of contentment he hadn't thought possible. Then he tugged at the belt of Eric's pants. "But I want these off."

"Mmm." Eric released his ass and cupped his jaw, guiding him up until their mouths met. The open kiss started slow, his tongue joining Eric's in a lazy dance, then a gentle tug on his lower lip, and he wanted to set that simmering passion free. He angled his head to deepen the kiss, ratchet it up to the next level, but Eric pulled back, easing his retreat with light quick kisses. "What about dinner?"

Bridge nuzzled into the groove of Eric's neck and breathed in that familiar cologne that was all Eric, all addicting, and kissed the slightly salty skin there. "Don't need food."

"But wait. Twenty bucks? Where'd you send them, McDonald's?"

Bridge huffed. Could the man just stop talking for five minutes? "God, you're a mouthy SOB."

"You like what I do with my mouth," Eric teased and reached down to cup Bridge's balls through his jeans, giving them a gentle but firm squeeze.

Bridge groaned—more like whined, if he were honest, because he would soon be in very real pain if he had to wait much longer—and rocked into the firm hold. "We've got enough time for a quickie before dinner, if you don't waste every second of it yapping away."

"You're such a romantic." Eric stepped back, and a seductive smile coaxed out Bridge's favorite dimple. Eyes locked on Bridge's, he finished unbuckling his pants, pulled the zipper, and gave his pants and underwear a shove down. Bridge could only stand still and soak in the sight of Eric standing before him, beautifully naked—save for the open shirt and jacket—and beautifully erect. Eric stepped out of the puddle of clothes at his feet and turned to retrieve them from the floor, spreading his legs as he bent down, and Bridge added *beautifully fuckable ass* to the list.

"I'm going to take a shower." Eric stood, faced him, and lifted an eyebrow. "You could use one too."

"Fuck," he whispered.

"Oh, we will." Eric walked backward slowly, fire blazing in his eyes. "But not before dinner."

Eric shifted in his seat and looked around the quaint restaurant while they waited for their meals to arrive. The lights were low, intimate, a candle centered on each table, and quiet Latin music drifted from speakers hung in the corners of the ceiling. No loud mariachi music to encourage a fun, party atmosphere here. There were couples at every single table. No families, no large parties of friends celebrating or coworkers decompressing after a long day at the office. Everything about this restaurant screamed romantic evening out.

When Bridge had suggested they go out for Mexican, Eric had expected something much more casual, buffet style even, because they were just friends out for a meal, not a couple out on a date.

Definitely not on a date.

*But a date would be nice, wouldn't it?* Eric forced back the errant voice with a shake of his head. He didn't want to want this. He couldn't want it. He'd just lose it in the end. Like always.

A boot nudged the side of his foot and slid up his calf, jerking him from the beginnings of a mild panic. He turned to find concerned eyes on him.

"Are you okay?"

"This is not a date." The words were out before Eric had even decided he was going to speak them. But they were right there on the end of his tongue and spilled out too quickly for him to corral.

Bridge blinked, sat back in his seat. "No. Of course not." He dropped his gaze and adjusted the silverware in front of him, like he meant to line them up just right, but not before Eric saw that normally warm, comforting gaze cool and detach. A needle of guilt threaded into his chest. Shit. He didn't want to end up hurt again, but he didn't want to hurt Bridge in the process of protecting himself either.

"Then what are we doing here, Bridge?" He lowered his voice, softened his tone. "Look around. It's all couples."

Bridge didn't meet his stare, just shrugged his shoulders in that way he did, like nothing could ever get to him, but Eric knew better. He'd seen the flash of disappointment in that open expression. He'd noticed the slight droop to Bridge's broad shoulders when he'd blurted out that this wasn't a date. Bridge had warned him from day one he'd want more, but Eric knew the easygoing cowboy would change his mind. When he did, Eric didn't want to find himself so far down the rabbit hole that he'd never be able to get back out again.

Bridge glanced up quickly, his voice lacking its usual vibrancy when he said, "They have the best enchiladas in all of Central California. That's all."

Silence fell between them, and Eric scrambled for a way to fill it, a way to get them back to their easy camaraderie. He reached for his sangria, taking a long draught to quench his dry throat, and the otherwise low din of murmured voices around them grew louder.

"I'd like to learn how to rope," he said a bit too loud. "If you were serious about teaching me."

Bridge looked up, his eyes searching for a second, and then the light returned to them, and he smiled. "I'm always serious."

"Liar."

Bridge grinned, and just like that the listing ship righted. "We can start tomorrow."

"Maybe you can teach me some knots that I can use to tie you up with later too."

Bridge's eyes widened, his cheeks pinked, and he opened his mouth—

"Here you are, guys." Angela, their server, who was completely unaware of how poor her timing was, lowered a plate of steaming hot enchiladas in front of each of them. "Can I get you anything else?"

Bridge still seemed speechless, which made Eric chuckle softly under his breath. "I think we're good here. Thank you."

With a practiced smile and nod, she left them to their meals, and Eric looked back at Bridge, who just shook his head. "You're an evil man, teasing me like that."

Eric raised his eyebrows. "Who said I was teasing?"

Bridge groaned and then dug into his dinner. Easy conversation followed while Bridge highlighted the finer points of roping and regaled Eric with tales of his misspent youth on the rodeo circuit. Eric had to admit, even though he'd been a bit freaked about the date-like setting of the restaurant, they did have the best enchiladas he'd ever tasted, and the company and conversion were completely enjoyable and relaxing. Maybe it wouldn't be so bad if this were a date. Dating could be casual—a step up from no-strings sex and a step down from a committed relationship. But he checked that thought. That road was all slippery slopes and man-sized potholes; it was too dangerous to navigate. Relationships only led to one thing: heartbreak.

More than two hours later, their plates were cleared, the check was delivered, and Eric felt like no time had passed at all. Which was both heartening and disconcerting.

"Come on. Let's get outta here." Bridge pulled his wallet from his back pocket, waving off Eric's attempt to snag the check, and tossed a few bills on top of it. "You're going to put out tonight, least I can do is buy you dinner."

Eric laughed. "There you go being all romantic again."

Bridge just waggled his eyebrows, and Eric gathered up his jacket and slid out of his chair. Expecting Bridge to have already started walking, leading the way out, he nearly collided with the big cowboy who stood like a brick wall staring at him. He leaned down, and Eric thought for sure Bridge was going to kiss him. Right there in the middle of the restaurant with everyone watching them. He didn't mind PDA in places where he felt safe enough—if he was on a real date or out with a boyfriend, neither of which this was.

"You're fucking gorgeous," Bridge whispered next to his ear. "I can't wait to get you naked again." Then he turned and walked away, casual as all get-out, like he hadn't just shorted all the wires in Eric's brain with that comment. Eric smiled and followed him outside. He couldn't wait either.

His smile was still there when he stepped up beside Bridge on the sidewalk in front of the restaurant, and the look he got in return was enough to make his knees weaken. Bridge reached out and clasped their hands together, lacing their fingers, and Eric froze. Panic rose in his chest even as he held on tighter.

"Friends don't do this," Eric said, an edge in his voice he couldn't hide.

"It doesn't have to mean anything. I just like touching you."

That voice, those eyes . . . *Damn you, Bridge.* It didn't have to mean anything, but deep down where he hid the things he didn't want to acknowledge, he knew it did. Yet he nodded anyway and relaxed his hand, because no matter how much he tried to deny it, it fucking felt right.

The walk back to Bridge's truck was short, and the streets were fairly quiet for a Friday night. But Folsom wasn't a big city known for its nightlife. Three men rounded a corner, approaching from the opposite direction, and scowls marred their otherwise unforgettable faces the very second the men noticed Eric and Bridge's clasped hands. He braced himself and sent a small prayer upward. Hopefully these guys weren't the type to do more than show their disapproval with their eyes.

Eric kept his gaze straight ahead. Bridge seemed oblivious. But the approaching men's stares were filled with so much baseless hate, it pricked at his skin, made him feel dirty, angry. He tried to pull his hand free again only for Bridge to give a reassuring squeeze. Did Bridge not realize what was going on here, what could happen?

They passed the trio without incident, if the man closest to Eric's side deliberately slamming his shoulder could be considered a non-incident. Bridge looked down at him then, the hard frown on his face out of character and looking very wrong on the normally unflappable cowboy.

Then one of the men tossed a slur back at them.

As far as antigay invectives went, it wasn't the worst Eric had ever heard, but that was beside the point. He'd long since learned to tune out any garbage spewing from the ignorant, uneducated, and simply mean-spirited. But he wasn't worried about himself right now. It was Bridge. Who'd tensed beside him and stopped dead in his tracks.

Shit.

Eric tried to pull his hand free again, only to have the grip around it tighten. Bridge rounded on the men, pulling up to his full, intimidating height.

"Bridge," Eric warned, tendrils of panic sliding into his chest. There was a time and place to confront, and it was not when outnumbered on a deserted street corner in the dark of night. "Leave it alone. They aren't worth it."

But Bridge didn't seem to hear him.

"Hey." The hard, sharp edge in Bridge's tone brought Eric up short. He'd heard the unfriendly way in which Bridge had spoken to Tripp last summer, when he'd thought Tripp was being an asshole to Marty, but that hadn't been anything to give him pause; it had only irritated him. This, though . . . Nothing compared to this dark, black sound coming from the man he associated with only light and laughter. "What did you just say?"

The three men turned around. The one in the middle looked pointedly down at their joined hands and then spat in their direction. "Ain't got nothing to say to the likes of you."

"Really?" Bridge gave Eric's hand a squeeze before letting go and stepping into the men's space. "Seemed you had a lot to say behind our backs a second ago. Why don't you come closer and tell me to my face?"

While Eric appreciated Bridge stepping up to defend them, he wasn't about to let the cowboy do it alone. He moved to stand shoulder to shoulder with Bridge, hands loosely fisted at his sides, stance widened, and eyes narrowed.

The men exchanged dubious glances with each other, and then Mr. Spitter spat again. This time the spray hit both their boots. He mumbled another string of tired slurs under his breath before the three of them turned and continued on at a brisk pace.

"Cowards." Bridge looked at Eric, that unreadable expression Eric was really starting not to like still on his face. Without another word, he took Eric's hand in his again and turned them back in the direction of the parking lot.

Silence followed them the rest of the walk back to the truck, and for the entire drive home. Eric couldn't think of what to say through the conflicting emotions warring inside his mind. Pride that Bridge had stood up to the bullies and had called them out on their bullshit. But fear danced with that ray of pride. Certainly after something like that, which would unfortunately happen again and again, Bridge would realize getting involved with a man wasn't worth it. Eric wasn't worth it. He hadn't been worth it for Jeremy or Ron. Hadn't been worth it for his parents. Hadn't been worth it for his foster parents . . .

So he kept his mouth shut and mentally prepared himself for what he knew would be coming. For Bridge to say he couldn't do this after all. He would be sorry and look heart stricken, and Eric would assure him it was okay and for the best. Bridge would thank him for understanding, and Eric would maintain a stoic expression. Then he would leave, drive down the road a few miles, and pull over to purge himself of the pain from once again hoping, attempting to believe, that he could have the one thing he was afraid to want most. Because as much as he'd tried to keep this thing with Bridge strings-free, he realized now that they'd already been too tangled up from day one. He'd never had a chance.

Kent was home when they arrived, sitting in the living room and talking on the phone. He wore a wide smile on his face, which meant it was probably Lily on the other end. For a brief second, Eric gave freedom to a rare flare of envy. No one would ever give a second glance at Kent and Lily walking hand in hand down the street. No one would ever spit at their feet. He quickly corralled that emotion, swallowing back that bitter pill. It would do him no good, and he couldn't—wouldn't—begrudge Kent any happiness. He was a good friend. At least he would be until Bridge kicked Eric to the curb and out of their tight circle. No matter what, if it came down to Bridge or Eric, Kent would chose Bridge. So would Marty and Tripp.

"Hey," Kent said, then did a double take when Bridge walked past without a word and went straight up the stairs to his room. The door closed with a quiet *snick* rather than the slam Eric had expected.

For a minute, Eric didn't know what to do. Grab his stuff and go home? Stay downstairs for a while to let Bridge work the incident out on his own? Or just head right on up there and get it over with so he didn't have to prolong the inevitable?

Kent looked at him then, his smile gone and an eyebrow lifted in question. No, he didn't want to stay down here and talk to Kent; he wanted to talk to Bridge. Now. He shook his head at Kent and followed his cowboy upstairs.

Two steps up he froze. *His* cowboy? Fuck.

What did he do now? Fight for it? Run from it? He'd fought for it before, but it had only hurt more when he'd lost.

Bridge was standing in front of the window when Eric entered the bedroom, staring out at what, he had no idea. The moonless night was pitch-black. Not even shadows played in the darkness. But he figured Bridge wasn't really seeing anything out there anyway.

Eric sighed and closed the door quietly behind him. Always the same. Why did he imagine things could be any different this time? All he could think to say was, "I'm sorry."

Bridge looked over his shoulder, brows furrowed, mouth tipped down in a frown. "Sorry for what? The only ones needing to say sorry are those assholes in town tonight."

"World's full of people like that," Eric said, looking around the room, his gaze falling on the messy bedsheets, bringing to mind the mess he and Bridge had made on the bed in the guest room the day before. But that was then, a brief interlude in a fantasy that had been shattered by another cold hammer of reality.

"I don't understand how anyone can be like that. What the fuck does it matter to them? They know nothing about us. You're one of the best men I've ever met, and I like to think I'm a pretty decent guy too. I try to be there for my friends and family. I work hard. I treat everyone with respect, whether I like them or not. That's the decent thing to do. What the fuck is it to them whose hand I hold or who I share my bed with? None of anyone's goddamn business."

"I'm sorry, Bridge." Eric sighed. "I don't have the answers you're looking for." He bent down to pick up his discarded work clothes from earlier, the ones he'd left on the floor when Bridge had hauled him into his en suite bathroom for an extra long shower before dinner. Hard to believe only a few short hours ago things had felt so right, but that was the way of it. Everything went to shit the moment he started letting his guard down, and he'd done a crap job of keeping it up around Bridge in the first place. That was clear as crystal now.

"What are you doing?"

Eric kept his head down, didn't want to meet Bridge's soulful eyes because he knew he wouldn't be able to carry on if he did. If Bridge said to stay, he would, because even now, he knew he couldn't say no to Bridge. "I should probably head on out."

"What the hell are you talking about?" Bridge stepped forward and stopped his movements with one hand on his wrist and the other under his chin, forcing him to look up.

Eric stepped back, out of Bridge's reach, and ignored the flash of hurt that streaked through his eyes. "What happened tonight? That was nothing. But it could have been so much worse and maybe next time it will be, because believe me, there will be a next time."

"You think I don't know that? My best friend is gay. People have tried to harass and bully him his whole life. Granted he didn't have it as bad as some, but it hasn't always been rainbows and puppies for him either. And don't think I've forgotten what Scott Gillard and his band of buzzards did to Tripp when he came out." Bridge stepped forward again, putting himself between Eric and the door so he would have to go around Bridge to get out. "And none of that should be any reason for you going home now."

"It has everything to do with it."

"I don't see how."

"No? Let me spell it out for you. I'm gay. You are not." Eric held up his hand when Bridge opened his mouth to argue. "You're bi . . . or bi-curious . . . Yeah, you fooled around once before, but you've never *really* been with a man before now. Since you dated women because you wanted to and not out of necessity, why subject yourself to this kind of grief by dating a man when you don't have to?"

"*Don't have to?*" The pitch in Bridge's voice raised a notch, as did the color in his face. "The hell kind of bullshit is that? I *have* to go with my heart, and my heart is going with *you*. That's where there's no choice. You could have three eyes and green skin for all I care. Issues with same-sex relationships are society's hang-up, not mine."

"It affects us too."

"Only if we let it." Bridge took a step forward. "I'm not going anywhere, Eric. I told you from the very beginning I wanted you more than as just a friend with benefits, and I don't give a shit what other people think or say or do, unless they hurt those I care about. That I won't stand for. But there is no way I'm not going to be with you because of other people's groundless issues. So you can get that shit out of your head right now, strip your damn clothes off, and get in my damn bed."

And then Bridge nodded, as if that put an immutable point on his tirade. The move was so . . . "so there," like a kid thinking that final nod held some sort of magic I-have-spoken-and-so-it-shall-be spell.

And so very Bridge. Eric couldn't stop the laughter that bubbled up out of nowhere and burst out into the silence cast over them by Bridge's enchantment, surprising them both.

"Not seeing the funny here." Bridge glared at him, and then his stare softened and he took a step forward. "You said dating."

"What?" Eric gripped the clothes in his hand tighter, like some sort of talisman. "No, I didn't."

"Yes. You said I didn't have to date a man if I didn't want to. But I do want to. I want to date you, Eric. I want us to have a real relationship. Please trust me when I say I'm not taking the old horse out for one last ride before sending him to pasture. The only thing I'm curious about is when you're going to believe that and let me in."

"It's not that, it's . . ." Eric dropped his gaze to the shirt he was strangling in his fists, and then Bridge's hand was on his cheek. Gentle, comforting, welcome. He hadn't even realized the man had moved, but there he was, guiding Eric up to meet those eyes that were starting to make him think just maybe . . . like that moment in the restaurant when he thought maybe dating would be okay.

"What is it?"

Eric sighed, closed his eyes for a second. "Relationships don't end well for me. Ever. You and the guys are the best thing I've had in my life in a long time, and I don't want to lose that."

Bridge closed the last bit of space between them, wrapping his arms around Eric, and Eric sank into him. There in that strong embrace was where he wanted to be. If they could stay like that, if time would stop right now, then the end would never come.

"Whatever happened in the past is the past. You can't let it dictate your future," Bridge said, one hand moving in soothing circles on Eric's back, the other cradling his head into the crook of Bridge's shoulder. "Will you think about it? Please?"

"Okay," he said, his voice a muffled whisper against Bridge's skin. Then he lifted his eyes up to meet Bridge's gaze. "I'll try."

"Thank you." Bridge leaned down and kissed him, slow and gentle, and it felt like a promise Eric wanted to believe.

Bridge meant for the kiss to be light, assuring, to let Eric know he was sincere but not pushing for more. He knew whatever was holding Eric back would eventually let go, but it would have to be at Eric's pace, not his. He eased off with a couple of soft nips at Eric's lips, and just as he was about to give Eric more room to decide what happened next, if anything, Eric dropped the clothes he'd been clutching between them and fisted a handful of Bridge's shirt.

He yanked Bridge to him so hard their chests crashed together, forcing a grunt from both of them. He pressed his open mouth to Bridge's, demanding entrance, which Bridge wasn't about to deny. Ever. He opened, and Eric dived in. Fuck, he loved the way the man kissed him. Passionate, desperate. Like it was their last day on earth, the last minute before the end of the world, and this final crushing kiss would be their final blaze of glory.

And it was sheer perfection.

"Fuck, you're hot all wound up like that," Eric said, and began to unbutton Bridge's shirt.

"Yeah?" A smile formed on Bridge's lips, and he playfully smacked Eric's hands away. He loved the aggressive side of Eric. "Get your ass in bed, and I'll show you how wound up I can get."

But instead of getting on the bed like he'd been told, Eric kissed him, hard, while he resumed divesting Bridge of his shirt. Bridge joined in, pushing the jacket off Eric's shoulders and then unbuttoning his shirt while their tongues danced and dueled for dominance. Buttons snapped, zippers screeched, clothes fell into hushed heaps without regard, and then all Bridge could feel was skin. Hot and smooth and sliding over flexing muscle that made his entire body sing halle-freakin'-lujah.

Eric broke the kiss and nipped at Bridge's neck. "Get on the bed." His voice was ragged and harsh, made more commanding by the thickened accent.

Bridge laughed at the switch, Eric now the one taking charge, but that simple display of power did things to him he couldn't really explain. He pulled the sheets back and crawled in, stretching out in the middle of the king-sized mattress, spreading his legs wantonly, and lacing his hands behind his head. His eyes never left the lithe, toned body before him as Eric dug in the drawer of the nightstand. For what, he had no idea.

"What am I supposed to have in there?"

Eric lifted an eyebrow, his expression dubious, like he wasn't sure if Bridge was teasing or not. "Condoms? Lube?"

"Oh. Well . . ." Bridge reached a hand out and ran it up Eric's firm, furred thigh. "I've never had a need for lube before, and I've never brought a woman home, so why have a stash here?"

"Never?"

Bridge ran through his memory quickly. *Huh.* "Nope. Anyone I dated never seemed to last beyond rodeo season. Oh! There's probably condoms in the RV still."

"Wow." Eric grabbed his pants off the floor and shook them out before stepping into them. "I think that's a bit sad, but it also turns me on that I'm the first lover you've brought home."

Unexpected warmth rushed through Bridge's body as the deeper meaning of that comment struck him. Eric was the first lover he'd ever brought home. *Lover?* The word popped in out of nowhere, but now that it was there, he liked it. Eric was his lover. "Yeah?"

"Yeah."

"So why are you putting clothes on?"

"To fetch supplies."

The guest room Eric had claimed was only two doors down, and he was back before Bridge even blinked, the hallowed supplies in his hands: a rather large bottle of lube and two boxes of condoms. Bridge raised his eyebrows when Eric rounded the side of the bed and placed them on the nightstand.

"Definitely not all for tonight," Eric said, grinning while slipping off his watch, negligently dropping it on the table beside the other items. He kicked out of his pants and crawled into bed, and Bridge wrapped his arm around Eric's shoulders, pulling him close.

"What are we doing with all of that?" Bridge had an idea, and that idea had his whole body vibrating, but he really didn't know what he was doing.

"You're going to fuck me."

"Jesus," Bridge croaked. Just like that, he was hard as a rock. "But I usually only fuck people I'm dating."

Eric held his gaze for a long moment, but Bridge couldn't get a read on what was happening behind those dark-blue orbs. They looked stormy, conflicted, but there was also something hopeful lurking there deep in the background. Finally Eric said, "Casual dating."

*Yes!* Bridge had the sudden urge to jump and pump his fists in the air, but he managed to maintain a modicum of control. Like dealing with a skittish horse, he just had to be patient until he earned Eric's trust. "So . . . you put out on the first date then?"

Eric smiled. "For you, maybe." He slid a hand down between their bodies and wrapped it around Bridge's straining dick. Bridge's eyelids fluttered, and a low keen whispered over his lips. Yes. He was never going to get enough of this—Eric in his arms, in his bed, playing him like a violin—and he rocked into the hold, leaning over to take Eric's mouth in a slow, teasing kiss. God, how he loved the feel of Eric's strong hand holding him, pleasuring him, owning him. And that's exactly what it was like. The man owned him, and he loved it.

The man he was now officially dating.

Eric broke the kiss, hand leaving Bridge's erection unattended to press at his shoulder, pushing him to his back. Eric crawled over him to straddle his hips, sliding forward to cradle Bridge's cock along the crack of his ass. This they had done before, and Bridge loved the tease of it, the promise of what that seductive groove held at its center, but now the tease was pushing him to the edge of his patience, and he wanted inside. Inside Eric. To be one with him, know him in every possible way, discover every nook and cranny and spot that made his eyes roll to the back of his head and stole his ability to speak.

Bridge lifted his hips to increase the pressure, create more friction, to tell Eric what he wanted without using words he couldn't form—that he was ready. But Eric arched forward, reaching behind to take Bridge in hand again, and the movement brought Eric's cock closer to Bridge's face. The train in his brain came damn close to derailing when it suddenly switched tracks.

"Give me," Bridge said softly, and licked his lips.

Eric paused. He sat so still that Bridge wondered if he was still breathing. When Eric finally spoke, his voice sounded restrained, a note of awe lingering beneath his sharp accent. "Are you sure?"

He might have made a fumbling mess of things last time, but this time he was going to do it right for Eric. "All guns bl—"

"Yeah, yeah. Waving all your guns like a madman." Eric laughed. "I got it."

"Let it ride, baby," Bridge said, and opened his mouth wide, waiting, watching the way Eric's pupils dilated and turned his eyes the color of a midnight sky. Then Eric smiled and knee-walked a few more inches up Bridge's torso, until the tip of his cock tapped the underside of Bridge's chin.

He stuck out his tongue, flattened it, and when the heavy weight of that long slender cock rested on it, his mouth immediately began to water.

He moved his head forward, marveling at the dichotomy of such hot, silken skin sliding over that hard column of flesh as it inched deeper into his throat. A tiny drop of pre-cum trickled free, and the bittersweet flavor of Eric's essence heightened his senses, bringing taste and smell and sound and touch into sharp focus. He closed his lips around Eric's cock so he could roll his tongue around the glans and swallow down that first heavenly flavor. And holy fuck, he had a dick in his mouth, and it tasted good, felt good, and might just be his new favorite thing to do. Especially when Eric watched him the way he did right now. Those intense, burning eyes, silently praising, encouraging, urging him on while at the same time leaving him in complete control of the pace and force.

And he wanted that praise. Needed it to know he was giving Eric as much pleasure as he could.

Bridge brought one hand up to grip the base of Eric's cock and cupped his ass with the other, using both to show Eric what he wanted. He sucked him deeper, until his lips met his fingers and the head of Eric's cock bumped against the back of his throat. But he was a long way from deep-throat ability, and his gag reflex forced him to pull back. Eric caressed Bridge's cheek, run his thumb along the edge of Bridge's mouth, and Bridge knew it was okay. He put extra effort into swirling his tongue around the tip, sucking on it like the unique lollipop it was, and then dove back down. At the same time, he pulled Eric forward, urging him to rock into his mouth, to use him, take his pleasure. And all the while Eric's gaze never wavered from his for even a split second.

Eric reached around, covered the hand Bridge currently was kneading his butt cheek with, and moved it toward his crack, guiding the fingers down until they met that tight pucker of enticing flesh. Bridge's pulse spiked, and he couldn't concentrate fully on the cock in his mouth, not when Eric used Bridge's fingers as an extension of his own—circling, massaging, adding pressure without breaching. Bridge didn't know if he was coming or going. He wanted to keep sucking, but he also wanted to slip inside that beautiful hole, into Eric.

His rhythm faltered and the hard flesh in his mouth was withdrawn, but his complaint stalled when Eric reached for the bottle of lube. His brain train switched tracks again. Eyes not straying from his, Eric popped the lid and leaned down to kiss him. Lost in the kiss, lost in Eric, he started when a dollop of cool, thick liquid landed on his busy fingers, slicking his ministrations.

"Open me," Eric whispered against his lips.

*Holy fuck.* No words for the cascade of emotion and desire and need that flooded through every inch of his body. This was really going to happen.

Hand now slippery with lube, Bridge pressed one finger inside Eric's body, and the tight heat that engulfed his digit burned through skin and muscle and bone, right into his very marrow. Jesus. Soon that would be his cock in there, sliding in and out of that smooth, wet channel.

A tremor rumbled through Eric and his eyelids fluttered, and a rush of pride raced through Bridge. He did that to the man above him, with his mouth, his hands, and hell if that wasn't a heady feeling. One he wanted to repeat again and again, to see how much higher he could push Eric into sheer ecstasy and beyond. Watch him shatter in rapture and glide back down to earth.

"Another." Eric gasped, and Bridge obeyed, fixated on the play of emotion on Eric's flushed face. Eric fucked himself on Bridge's fingers, pushing them deeper and deeper until Bridge was buried to his knuckles.

"Christ, Eric." Bridge panted. "This is so . . . You are so . . . fucking hot."

"Time to save a horse," Eric said. He grabbed a box of condoms from the table, tore it open with his teeth, pulled out one foil package and opened that with his teeth as well, and then, reaching around, he slowly covered Bridge's hard, aching length with it.

Bridge carefully pulled his fingers free, eliciting a quiet groan from Eric, then Eric wrapped his hand around the base of Bridge's cock and pressed the head against his hole, pausing there for just a breath. Then he began to slowly, maddeningly, lower himself down Bridge's length, inch by inch, until Bridge was fully seated inside the gorgeous man.

*Inside him.*

He had to pause and let the thought, the sensation, the reality settle in for a few heartbeats. Nothing in his life could compare to this complete joining with Eric, and he had a feeling nothing ever would again. Sure, it wasn't his first time having sex, not even his first time with anal, but it was his first time with Eric and that made all the difference. Because he was buried in Eric and he loved how right and perfect that felt.

His instincts screamed at him to move, to thrust, to claim, but he didn't know who should start, and a slow shiver skimmed over the surface of his skin, leaving goose bumps in its wake. "Can we move now?"

"Hellya."

Eric rose and quickly set a steady rhythm, up and down, in and out, riding Bridge's cock from tip to base and back, until the pace became too measured and Bridge needed more. He gripped Eric's lean hips, holding him in place so he could thrust up into that tight heat with abandon. Eric braced himself with both hands on Bridge's chest, fingers digging into his skin, under it, creating permanent holds, and Bridge hoped he'd be branded for life.

"There you go," Eric murmured and rocked back, meeting Bridge's upshot with enough force that the slap of meeting skin echoed in the room around them, fighting for control of an invisible battlefield with harsh, erratic breaths and wordless grunts. It was loud and messy and fierce, and he loved every fucking second of it.

Eric took himself in hand and began stroking rapidly, gaze locked on Bridge's mouth. Bridge's whole body tightened, preparing for what he already knew was going to be a mind-blowing orgasm. His balls pulled up close, and sparks of electricity gathered in his groin, at the base of his shaft. He raced for the gate but fought back to stop from reaching it so soon. He wanted to come, to explode, to shout his release loud enough for the whole world to hear, but he didn't want it to end. He wanted to ride out this sharp edge as long as possible so he'd never have to leave this tiny private corner of heaven, the one that belonged only to him and Eric.

But the outcome of the battle left his hands the second Eric's muscles squeezed hard around his cock. His breath caught in his throat, and his release shot from him like an angry Brahma out of the chute. Snorting, grunting, twisting, crushing—the most amazing fucking ride of his life. Eric rode the edge of Bridge's orgasm, hand flying faster on his cock, bottom lip pulled into his mouth, but his eyes were still locked on Bridge's, almost like he was begging for word from him to let go.

"Yeah, babe," Bridge said. "Come on me."

Eric's head fell back on his shoulders, his mouth dropped open, and the growling whine of relief that escaped from him sent a shower of excitement raining over Bridge's overheated skin. Hot streams of cum splattered his stomach until his sexy New Yorker had spent himself and collapsed on top of him.

Bridge wrapped his arms around Eric, holding him close while their hearts continued to pound, ragged breaths scraped over dry throats, and sweaty skin cooled.

"Just when I think it can't get any hotter, it gets hotter."

Eric didn't seem capable of more than a short chuckle into the crook of Bridge's neck, and after a few minutes, he sat up and eased off Bridge. He removed the condom and glanced around for somewhere to toss it.

"Floor," Bridge said, and Eric raised an eyebrow at him.

"You're not in college anymore, Dorothy." He kissed Bridge and then got up. "Be right back."

Bridge stared at the play of muscle flexing in that firm ass as Eric crossed the room before he disappeared in the en suite to discard the used condom. When he returned, he had a small bucket with him. "For next time."

*Next time.* Bridge liked the sound of that.

Eric set the trash bin beside the night table and then picked up his work shirt from the floor. He climbed back onto the bed, straddling Bridge again, and began wiping his drying cum from both of their stomachs.

Bridge smiled up at Eric, enjoying watching the man tend to them and the companionable silence that settled between them. He glanced over his shoulder, reached for his cowboy hat that hung on the bedpost, and plopped it on Eric's head. "There, now you're a real cowboy."

Eric grinned. He tossed the shirt back on the floor and adjusted the hat to sit lower on his brow. "Told you I knew how to ride."

# CHAPTER
## NINE

Eric shifted in the saddle. The leather seat was a little too hard for his little-too-tender ass. It had been a long time since he'd bottomed, and Bridge was . . . well proportioned to his build. Big. He smiled. That dull ache was a sweet reminder of last night's romp.

"What's with the smile?" Bridge watched him with curious eyes as they rode side by side back to the barn. After spending a good hour earlier that morning learning from Bridge how to lasso a plastic steer head attached to a bale of hay, he'd decided they should take a ride on a nearby trail. The first half hour had been exactly as Eric had imagined riding the range would be like. Just them, their horses, and the Wild West stretched out for miles around them. The steady beat of hooves, the creak of leather, and the warm floral spring breeze worked like a balm to his soul—cleansing every worry, every concern, every doubt. Even his doubts about agreeing to date Bridge didn't seem so big. Casual was still strings-free, right? Casual was still open. It didn't mean he . . . what? Didn't mean they were boyfriends, didn't mean they were in a relationship. He could still avoid the coming heartbreak if he didn't let himself fall deeper than that.

Right?

The mental silence that came back to him was more unnerving than the little voice arguing with him.

He shook himself free of thoughts that were making him crazy. Right here, right now, he had a little piece of heaven, and for the first time in his life, he felt truly at peace. For now, he could let all that fall by the wayside and be in this moment.

But he wasn't used to riding, and by the end of the second half hour, things were getting uncomfortable, and all he wanted was to get his feet back on the ground.

"I need to get out of this saddle and off this horse," Eric said.

Bridge cocked his head. "And that makes you smile?"

"No, the reason why I'd rather not be sitting on this hard seat anymore does."

Color rose in Bridge's cheeks, and he glanced away. "That was amazing," he said quietly. He looked over and met Eric's gaze with that demure bravado Eric found so fascinating and endearing. "I want to try that too."

Eric grabbed the horn of the saddle, holding on through the sudden wave of light-headedness as all his blood ran southward. "When you're ready," he managed, trying to get a grip on himself before he really did fall off this damn horse. Yes, he wanted that. Who wouldn't? But he'd never really imagined Bridge would want to.

"I'm ready."

Eric closed his eyes, groaning. "Killing me here."

Bridge reached out and squeezed his knee and then pulled his horse ahead as they rounded the barn. Kent was standing by the gate that led into the main yard and opened it for them when they approached.

"What's up, dude?" Bridge asked as he cleared the gate and hopped down from his horse.

"Your mom called."

Bridge's cheeks paled slightly, and a guilty expression took over his face. "Uh-oh."

"Yeah, uh-oh." Kent closed the gate behind Eric and secured the chain. "She's a little pissed you haven't called her back yet. Did you forget about tomorrow?"

Eric glanced between Bridge and Kent. "What's tomorrow?"

"My birthday," Bridge said, his tone casual, like he should have known.

Eric's eyebrows shot up, and he sucked in a harsh breath. "Your what?"

"I thought I told you last weekend." Bridge came around to stand beside Rosie, waiting while he threw a leg over her back to dismount. "It's not a big deal. Just us, Kent, Marty and Tripp, and my family for dinner and the mandatory birthday cake."

Eric knew all the color had drained from his face by the way his skin suddenly felt too tight and his scalp crawled. His feet hit the ground and his legs, which had somehow turned to rubber during the course of their ride, just about gave out. Bridge had apparently anticipated it, though, because a large hand was at the small of his back, offering support while he settled on solid ground again. "Us?"

Bridge frowned and glanced at Kent, who frowned in return.

"Yeah. Of course." Bridge looked to him and then back to Kent, like he was silently asking for help, but there didn't seem to be much guidance in Kent's shrug. "You want to go, right? Shit. I didn't even think. I'm sorry. I figured you—"

"No. I . . ." Eric looked down at the reins in his hands, fidgeted with them for a second. How did he tell Bridge he couldn't do family dinners? Couldn't do family? His voice softened when he said, "I didn't know. I . . . I don't have a gift."

"Oh, don't worry about that." Bridge draped an arm over Eric's shoulder and pulled him close. "You'll be giving me your gift later, when we get home."

"Oh God." Kent held a hand up. "I don't want to know. My gift to you is the house to yourselves. I'll sleep in the rig."

Kent and Bridge laughed, but Eric remained quiet, and without a word or look back, he slipped out from under Bridge's arm and led Rosie to the barn.

"What happened there, Eric? Did I do something wrong?"

He started at Bridge's deep voice right behind him a few minutes later, so lost in his thoughts, he hadn't even heard him approach. He didn't turn around, just kept running the brush over Rosie's shiny coat. "No! No, it's okay. I was just . . . You know . . . A bit of warning would have been appreciated."

"I'm sorry. I swear, I thought I'd told you last weekend." Bridge must have picked up a brush too, because he stepped into the stall on Rosie's other side and began grooming the docile mare with long, slow strokes. "I'm so used to how tight our families have always been and forgot that not everyone has the same thing."

Eric couldn't raise his eyes to meet Bridge's. Not yet. It was embarrassing enough to find out the cowboy's birthday was the following day and to be completely unprepared. How had he not known? Why hadn't anyone told him? More than that, why hadn't he asked? And meeting the family . . .? That freaked him out even more. Wasn't that what couples who were serious about taking their relationships to the next level did? Introduce the significant other for approval? He'd only agreed to move from no strings to dating just last night. *Casual* dating. They were nowhere near the meet-the-family stage, and he doubted they'd even reach that point. Not to mention, no family would approve of him anyway. If he'd been worthy enough, his own family would never have given him up in the first place.

Which led to another worrisome thought.

"Do they know?" Eric risked a glance at Bridge, who frowned.

"Does who know what?"

"Your family. They know you're bisexual?"

"Oh."

*Oh? Great.* Instead of a double whammy it was a trifecta.

Silence hung thick in the space between them while he watched Bridge, who looked lost in thought as he chewed on his lower lip, gaze following the hand that Eric groomed Rosie with. She snorted and swished her tail, the ends snapping Eric's bare forearm.

Then Bridge shrugged one shoulder, and for the first time, Eric found the habit irritating rather than endearing. Bridge lifted his eyes, and that warm gaze settled on Eric. He smiled. "No time like the present. I'll call them when we get back to the house."

Eric's heart jumped into his throat, and he gasped. "What?"

"It's okay. They'll be fine with it. Then it'll all be out in the open before we get there."

"How can you be so sure?" *How can you be so frustratingly nonchalant?*

"Because they love Marty like their own."

"But you *are* their own. That's different."

Bridge paused his strokes and rested his arm on Rosie's back, regarding him for a long moment. "Do you know why Marty, Kent, and I are practically brothers? Our parents are best friends. They're all ranchers who grew up valuing family above all else, and family sticks together, no matter what. They also believe in the 'it takes a village to raise a child' thing, so when something happens to one of their friends' kids, it happens to all of them. They might have to revise what they envisioned for my future, but they'll still be beside me regardless."

"I don't know." Eric tore his eyes from Bridge, staring at Rosie's muscular shoulder while he brushed. From his experience, things that sounded too good to be true usually were. He didn't understand how these guys, their families, could be so open and accepting, how Bridge could simply expect that. The whole concept was foreign to him. "Maybe you should wait."

"For what?"

"You know, to be sure this is what you want before you go telling them something that big."

"Oh." That one word, delivered like a punch to the solar plexus, brought Eric's attention back to Bridge. The gold flecks in Bridge's gaze dimmed, his usual warmth cooled, and he lowered his head, hiding behind the brim of his hat. "You still think I'm going to wake up and realize I'm riding the wrong horse? Or that I'm going to dump you like people in your past have?"

*Yes.* But he couldn't say that, not when the hurt in Bridge's voice was his doing. "No. Just . . ."

"Eric, I know it probably seems fast. I mean, until a couple of weeks ago, you thought I was straight. But we've known each other almost a year now. I've been dreaming about you for months, and this is not a whim or a temporary fling. Not for me."

Eric sighed, dropped the brush into the tack box sitting by stall door, and walked around Rosie to stand beside Bridge. "I'm sorry. You're right. I just haven't had the same experiences. That's all. I don't know why my family tossed me away. The one family I told I was gay couldn't send me back fast enough." He copied Bridge and shrugged his shoulder. "It'll be fine. I was caught off guard."

Bridge turned and wrapped his strong arms around Eric's waist, pulling him in close. He melted into the embrace, wanting nothing more than to stay right there for the rest of his life. If time didn't move, then things couldn't fall apart.

"I'm sorry they did that to you. I'd feel sorry for them if I weren't so pissed off at them for what they did to you. They are the ones who lost out on getting to know what an amazing, giving man you are. But

I'm not them. I'm not going to walk away from you." Bridge's warm, moist breath fanned lightly over his neck, and Eric wanted so badly to believe him. *You can.*

"And I'm sorry I assumed you'd be fine with going," Bridge continued. "That was thoughtless of me. We don't have to go, if you don't want to. It's not a big deal."

"No," Eric said, with more bravado than he felt. "It's your birthday, and that is a big deal. We'll go. It'll be good."

# CHAPTER
## TEN

T he very next night, Eric sat in a comfortable chair at a long table set for fourteen instead of the seven he'd expected—and that was only for the adults. There was another table set for five kids. He'd been so very wrong: this was not all good.

"Just us" turned out to be him and Bridge, the guys, and Bridge's family consisting of his parents, grandparents, two older brothers and their wives, and five pint-sized Sullivans ranging from three to twelve years old, who were currently wreaking havoc on the household. And the whole damn family was big and blond. Like they'd descended from Vikings rather than cowboys.

To say he was overwhelmed would be an understatement.

Bridge's parents had been nothing but warm and welcoming, though, making him feel as if he were already a part of their family. After meeting them, it was no secret where Bridge got his warmth. Not a single member of the Sullivan clan gave him a sideways look or skipped a beat when Bridge had introduced him as his date. His *date*! He'd felt a rush of equal parts joy and terror at the claim, but the family came at him from every direction—a constant swell of motion and sound—making it hard to dwell. Mr. and Mrs. Sullivan insisted he call them Hank and Lenora, and Bridge's grandparents demanded to be addressed as Abe and Willa. The brothers, Bill and Barrett, were both ranchers. The oldest, Barrett, had his own spread, and Bill lived on and worked the family ranch.

Eric sat between Bridge and Barrett, marveling at the camaraderie and obvious love the family shared, wanting to be a part of it but unsure how without losing himself to them completely. They made it hard for him to keep his guard up, what with Lenora fussing over him to eat more, Abe topping his glass of wine so it never dipped below half full, and the brothers and their wives, Angie and Joan, peppering him with questions about his career and New York and how he managed to put up with Bridge's nonsense, which led to a round of good-natured ribbing and more carefree laughter.

And therein lay the problem.

He liked all of them and could too easily become attached to this big, boisterous family. It scared the hell out of him. Made him want to burrow into their fold and never leave, while at the same time, his feet itched to get up and run fast and far, before it all went to hell. As much as he wanted a life like this, he knew he was just one of those people for whom it was never meant to be.

A cold sliver of panic tickled across his chest. Disposable people didn't get to keep lives like this. He needed to get out now, before he got in any deeper and the curb would hurt too much. He was already in too deep, knew it was going to hurt anyway, but he could limit the damage if he just ended it right now, on a high note while they could still take good memories with them.

A warm hand settled on his thigh and squeezed slightly. He turned to find Bridge looking at him closely, his gaze searching. And all Eric's worry that things would fall apart and his resolve to end things on his terms faded away under that concerned stare. He couldn't walk away from this, from Bridge. Soon he'd have to, but not yet.

"Are you okay?" Bridge whispered while the chaos that was the Sullivan clan carried on around them.

Eric didn't know how to put what he was feeling into words, but now wasn't really the time for it anyway. He plastered on his best smile and nodded. "They're just so . . ."

"Yeah." Bridge chuckled. "They can be a bit much, I guess. But I told you they'd be good with us, right?"

"Yeah. I can't even believe how much of a nonissue that is."

Bridge practically preened. "That's my family."

"It's not that though. It's . . ." He trailed off, glancing around the table at the happy faces of a family completely at ease with each other.

Bridge leaned in closer. "What is it?"

"I don't know how to do this," he confessed.

"This?"

Eric answered with a shrug. Bridge seemed to understand because he didn't press for more. He just slid that hand a little higher up Eric's thigh, sending a rush of blood to his groin, and kissed his cheek. "We stick together and help each other through whatever comes our way," Bridge said. "That's how." The promise in his voice was so clear it made Eric's eyes sting.

And then Eric's heart about blasted a hole through his rib cage when an earsplitting whistle rent the air, silencing the table and bringing everyone to sharp attention. Lenora stood in the doorway that led from the dining room to the kitchen, holding a massive cake, tall candles flickering gold and yellow under her chin. And, as if they'd been counted in by a conductor, the family launched into a perfectly harmonized rendition of "Happy Birthday."

"Make a wish!" Marty shouted.

"And blow hard," Bill teased, eliciting a round of laughter from the table, a groan and eye roll from Bridge, and a flood of heat into Eric's cheeks. Bridge turned to him then, his smile turning sly. He winked before inhaling pretty much all of the oxygen in the room and blew out all twenty-nine candles in one long exhalation. He sat back, looking mighty proud of himself, while everyone laughed, and Lenora set about cutting slices of dense chocolate cake onto small plates. Willa then scooped vanilla ice cream on top of each, and then Angie passed them on down the table until they all had a plate in front of them.

"What'd you wish for, little bro?" Bill asked, his grin so much like Bridge's.

"Secret." Bridge shot a quick glance at Eric. "But it'll be coming true tonight."

"I can't believe you told them that," Eric said when they climbed into bed later that night.

"What?"

"About your wish? 'It'll be coming true tonight.'" Eric mimicked Bridge's voice, and except for the accent, Bridge couldn't deny he'd done a pretty good job of it. "You may as well have just come right out and said we're having sex."

"It's not like anyone would think otherwise." Bridge pulled him into his arms and kissed him soundly, rolling them until he was draped over Eric's leaner frame. "I think it's time for my present now."

"How do you want me, birthday boy?"

Bridge stared at him for a long moment. He'd been dreaming about this for a long time, wondering what it would be like, and then after seeing how much Eric had loved it . . . He was ready for it. "I want you to fuck me."

Eric's eyes darkened, desire burned in them. "God, are you su—"

"Don't make me say it," Bridge teased.

Eric chuckled, and the sound drifted into a moan. "I'm going to give you the best birthday gift of your entire life."

"That's what I'm hoping for, stud."

"Roll onto your stomach."

He made quick work of doing as Eric bid, and his body began to shake with excitement and anticipation of what was to come. He loved the way he'd made Eric squirm and writhe in pleasure when he'd made love to him and couldn't wait to be on the receiving end, and— Fuck. He hadn't fucked Eric the other night; that hadn't been just sex. He'd made love to him. *Love.* Because . . .

*I love him.*

And trailing that thought came a sense of rightness unlike any he'd ever felt before, something inside him lifted, opened, and even though it was nighttime, the sky suddenly seemed lighter, the room warmer.

*I am. I'm in love with Eric Palmer. Holy hell.*

"Bridge?"

"Uh, yeah?" Bridge coughed and buried his head in the pillow for a second. When he turned to meet Eric's gaze, the man looked different somehow. His features smoother, his eyes brighter, the way his mouth curved when he smiled more enticing, and the hint of a dimple in his left cheek—the one that never quite materialized, but lurked beneath the surface nonetheless—intriguing. Everything about him was . . . beautiful. And it was more than how he looked. It was the sound of his voice and that sharp accent that grew thicker when he was turned on; the way he always seemed to make sure Bridge was happy, satisfied; and the care he gave when sharing new experiences with him. The way he looked out for people and went beyond just fixing their wounds.

The way he simply made Bridge feel alive.

*I love you.*

"Kiss me," Bridge whispered, stretching to meet Eric for a slow, promising caress of mouths, and then Eric smoothed a hand down Bridge's back while shifting to nip at his shoulder. The hand dropped to the crack of his ass, while wet lips trailed along the curve of his spine. Fingers rubbed gently against his hole, and lazy kisses trickled down to meet them. Every single touch seemed infused with fire, every single kiss an electric charge, and every sensation greater and more powerful than the last. He jumped when a hot, wet tongue traced around his opening, darting just inside.

"Holy Jesus." Bridge gasped. That was something he could get used to. "Do that again."

Eric chuckled. "Your wish . . ." And then that strong slippery muscle slid through the crack of his ass, circling and dipping into his hole, and sent shivers cascading over his skin. It was too much and not enough, but all he knew was that he wanted more. He wanted Eric to own him completely tonight, and he couldn't wait another second for it to start.

"Now," he growled.

Eric chuckled. "Not even close, cowboy. I won't chance hurting you just because you're too damned impatient."

"Cruel man."

"You'll be singing my praises before you know it."

Bridge started to speak, but a strong finger pushed inside and froze the air in his lungs. For the first time, Eric had breached him, and the reality of what was soon to come heightened his senses into acute awareness centered completely on his ass and what was happening to it. Eric's cock was going to be in there. Frightening. Exciting. His whole body shook with anticipation.

In and out the finger worked, sometimes joined by that talented tongue, and together they raised his pleasure to another level. Step-by-step, his need for more rose. Deeper and deeper Eric pushed, wider and wider he opened, and then pressure on something inside sent an explosion of blinding sparks blasting in every direction. "Holy . . . hell . . ."

"You like?"

Bridge panted. Laughed. "God yes. Do that again."

Finally, after what seemed like hours, when Bridge couldn't take another second of being on the edge Eric had him riding with fingers and tongue, he removed both and left Bridge empty, open, and the most vulnerable he'd ever felt in his life. But Eric would take care of him. He knew without a doubt that he was safe with this man he'd fallen hard for. Probably had fallen for a long time ago and had just not realized it.

He distantly registered the pop of a lid and the tearing of a condom wrapper, and then blunt pressure against his hole drew his complete and absolute attention. Eric's cock.

Fuck.

Would it hurt? Would he love it or hate it? He had no idea what to expect, only the tease of what Eric's fingers had felt like inside of him, but he wanted it. More than he'd ever thought possible.

Eric rocked his hips gently, slowly, incrementally pushing himself inside, and Bridge gasped at the acute spike of pain, tried to pull away.

"Easy," Eric said, his voice low and soothing, and that rumbling accent washed over him like a caress. A hand moved in slow circles on his back, calming, assuring. "Try to breathe and think about relaxing your body."

Bridge nodded, unable to speak right then. He didn't see how he was going to be able to take all of Eric, but he was damn well going to try. He wanted this; he just had to do what Eric said. Slow down and relax. When he did, his muscles loosened up enough for the head of Eric's dick to breach him, and he tensed again at the ache and burn, but below that was another sensation—something he'd never felt before, something better.

"That's it," Eric crooned. "Keep breathing."

The pain began to ebb, and as it faded, he chased the burn that replaced it. It was a weird edge, a sweet mix of pleasure and agony, and then heaven when he realized Eric's cock was inside of him. All the way. Stretching him, filling him, each gentle thrust pushing him deeper inside until Bridge was certain he'd pierce his heart. Eric stopped, letting Bridge adjust to the new sensations, and his heightened senses recorded every single thing. The way his whole channel felt deliciously full, the way the hard flesh throbbed inside him, the incredible heat of it, how Eric's pelvis was flush against his ass and heavy balls rested against his. He felt it all, right down to the subtle tremble of Eric's body as he struggled to hold still, waiting for Bridge to drop the flag that signaled a green light, and the breath Bridge couldn't quite seem to catch.

Bridge hooked a hand behind him, reaching to grab a handful of Eric's firm ass, and tugged him closer, trying to get Eric deeper, but Eric pulled back, almost all the way out, before thrusting back in. The head of his cock slid over that spot inside his body that stole his breath, blowing out his vision on every stroke.

Never in all his life could he have imagined how amazing this could feel. Yeah, he loved fucking Eric, but holy hell. He just might want to bottom all the time.

It felt so good. No, not good. Incredible, amazing, mind-blowing . . . Nope, none of those words came close, either. Having Eric inside of him, owning him, loving him was well and truly beyond description. He wanted more, always, even as he knew he wouldn't last much longer, but he didn't want to come this way, with his face in the pillow. "Wait, stop."

Eric stopped immediately. "Are you okay? Did I hurt you?" Worry laced his rough voice.

"No, no." Bridge turned his head so Eric could read the truth in his eyes. "This is so fucking beyond-words awesome, but I want to face you when I come."

"Jesus, Bridge." Eric leaned down for a kiss. "You're fucking incredible." Eric carefully pulled out and rolled Bridge to his back, lifting his legs and draping them over Eric's sturdy shoulders, and then he lined up and plunged back inside.

"God, yes!" Bridge's eyes rolled into the back of his head; he wondered how the hell sex with Eric kept getting better, how every single time could possibly be better than the last. But it was. Every. Single. Time.

The pace quickened, Eric's thrusts short and fast, and then he slowed down, pushing all the way in and slowly pulling all the way out. Fast or slow, short or deep, it was sweet heaven, and soon Bridge was skirting the point of no return. He took his cock in hand and started to stroke hard and fast, matching Eric's rhythm.

"Soon, soon, soon," he panted. Eric's hand covered his, and together they brought him over the edge.

His release spilled onto his stomach in scalding jets, and seconds later, Eric growled above him, grinding out his release and pushing so deep inside Bridge that he was certain they'd fused together and become one. They stayed that way, frozen in the aftermath of ecstasy, shuddering in its wake.

"Take a breath," Eric said, his voice a low rasp. Bridge did, wincing as Eric carefully pulled out. "Okay?"

"Okay."

Eric tossed the condom in the trash bin and then leaned down and kissed Bridge, short and sweet because they hadn't yet recovered enough breath for more. Eric settled in beside him, and Bridge reached out, found Eric's hand, and twined their fingers together.

"From now on, every day is my birthday."

Eric laughed. "Well, I wouldn't mind having a birthday once in a while too."

Bridge turned to look at Eric, loving the spent, sated expression, the contented glow in his eyes. Just fucking loving him. He ran a finger along the line of Eric's jaw and then leaned in and kissed him, slow and thorough and infused with all the love he felt inside. When he pulled back, a funny expression crossed Eric's handsome features, too fleeting for Bridge to identify.

"Happy birthday, cowboy," Eric said quietly.

"Best birthday gift ever. By far." Bridge closed his eyes, a smile still holding his cheeks up as he drifted off into peaceful slumber.

# CHAPTER
## ELEVEN

The first thing Eric was aware of, when consciousness began to creep back in, was a large warm hand resting on his hip, even breathing close by, and roosters crowing in the distance. He lifted his eyelids to find Bridge smiling down at him, hair mussed in a sexy fashion and a playful light shining from those inviting chocolate-colored eyes.

"Good morning, stud," Bridge said, his voice rough with sleep and arousing as hell.

"Mornin'. How are you feeling?"

"Perfect. A little sore, but it was so worth it." Bridge leaned forward and kissed him. Just a warm press of lips, familiar and comfortable. "I got something for you."

"Yeah?" Eric stretched and smiled as a callused hand slid down his hip and ghosted his groin. A finger teased along his waking flesh and came to rest flat on his stomach. "Is it my birthday now?"

"Soon, but first." Bridge rolled away and leaned over the side of the bed. Eric heard paper rustle, a grunt from Bridge, and then he sat back up with a dark-brown cowboy hat and a pair of intricately stitched snakeskin boots in his hands. "Your very own."

Eric stared at the gifts, and then at Bridge. The look in those eyes . . . It was the way he'd seen Marty and Tripp look at each other. The way Kent looked at Lily. Even as it sent a thrill spreading through his body and loosened something in his chest, a distant clang of bells also rang in his head because it couldn't possibly be real. He wouldn't name that look. Couldn't. If he did, he'd jinx it and history would repeat itself once again.

But the way Bridge smiled at him . . . like he was someone worth that word he wouldn't even think, let alone voice . . .

*God, Eric. Get a grip. It's just a gift, not a declaration. Nothing to freak out over.*

He forced back the doubts and fears that had cluttered his mind for too long and sat up, taking the hat from Bridge so it rested in his lap. "When did you get these?" *And why?*

"When you were at work the other day. Well, I had to wait for them to ship the boots in from another store, so I had Kent pick them up yesterday."

"Thank you," Eric said, his voice sounding rough to his own ears. "They're beautiful."

"The boots should fit. I checked the size of your work boots, but we can go back if they're not right."

"I can't believe you got these for me."

"A cowboy without his boots and hat is like that nightmare where you forget to put your clothes on and you're standing out in public stark-naked."

Eric laughed, and Bridge leaned over to run a finger along the curve of his jaw, and then he kissed him, a slow savoring of lips, a teasing slide of tongue, and a word Eric didn't want to give life to.

Bridge pulled back and looked at him with that searching, too-warm gaze again. His voice too soft, too intimate, when he spoke. "Eric, I . . ."

*No, no, no. Please don't say it.*

"I was wondering . . . What do you think about staying in my rig for rodeo season? With me?"

"What?" The word choked out of his mouth, a tremor rattled down his spine, and a strange sense of disappointment seeped into the back of his mind. Why on earth *not* hearing the unspeakable word had caused that reaction, he refused to examine. He didn't *want* to hear it. Did he? No. No, he did not. That word was a harbinger of heartbreak.

Bridge sat up, and the bedsheet pooled in his lap. "Well, your little Tonka truck camper is too small for us, and in mine, we'd have the closest thing to a real bedroom on the road. I do have a full-sized queen in there, so it kind of makes sense."

"But, I-I need my truck."

Bridge's mouth dipped down a touch at the edges. "Well, yeah. For work and all, but at night, we could share my trailer."

Eric nodded his head once. He supposed it did make sense to sleep in the bigger rig since they'd never be able to share the actual bed in his camper. If he could look at it that way instead of as another foot deeper into the rabbit hole . . . "What about Kent?"

The small frown Bridge wore righted itself, and a mischievous glint sparkled in his eyes. "Dude, I'm never going to agree to a threesome."

Eric just shook his head. "Not what I meant."

"Yeah, I know. If he gets tired of your screams of ecstasy every night, he can go sleep in your camper."

Eric fought back a smile. He appreciated Bridge's attempt to lighten the mood, keep him from overthinking, but he had too many reservations. He looked down at the hat in his lap, ran a finger along the edge of the brim. "I don't know. It seems kind of . . ."

Bridge tucked a finger under Eric's chin and forced him to look up and meet the dark gaze that promised a future and felt like home and made him want to run away for the very same reasons. Eyes that banked hurt in their depths while they quietly asked for trust.

"I'm not asking you to move in. Yet. We just started dating." Bridge smiled. "But if things keep going like I think—hope—they will, maybe you'll consider it at the end of the season."

*Yes!*

*No!*

Eric forced himself to breathe, to slow down and think while his heart sang with joy, but the little voice in the back of his mind reminded him this couldn't last.

If he accepted Bridge's offer to share his trailer, and if Bridge hadn't kicked him out by season's end—which he knew was unlikely since he was usually shown the door within a year—he knew he would move all the way in with Bridge. But as thirty years of experience had taught him, Bridge would reach the point everyone else had and dump him. Then where would he be? He wouldn't even have his own house to retreat to.

He forced a smile he hoped looked relaxed while in the back of his mind he cataloged where all his belongings were and how fast he could get out of the house without offending Bridge. "Can I think about it?"

Bridge studied him for a long moment, and Eric fought back the urge to blurt out that he didn't actually need to think on it. Bridge's expression saddened for a flash, and then he smiled a bit too big. "Of course! Take your time. I was just, you know, throwing it out there."

Bridge took the cowboy hat from Eric's hands and gently placed it on his head. "Perfect." He kissed him quickly and then hopped out of bed. "C'mon, let's get breakfast. I'm starving."

Bridge threw his coils and missed the horns of the plastic steer head fastened to a bale of hay. Again. He couldn't focus on practicing his lasso techniques with his mind so stuck on replaying the last kiss he'd shared with Eric. He'd hoped the practice would help him take his mind off how that kiss had somehow felt like a good-bye instead of a *how will I survive the next five days without you*. But so far, he was only getting more and more frustrated.

"Eric working today?" Kent finally spoke. Bridge had heard the dull *thud* of hoofbeats on hard-packed dirt a short while ago. Knew by the creak of leather and stamp of a foot on the ground that Kent was sitting astride his horse watching, but Bridge didn't acknowledge him in any way, just kept throwing useless coils at the plastic steer.

"Nope." Bridge tossed and missed. "Went back to Redding early. Said he had a lot to do in prep for the season start this weekend."

"Yeah, looks like you do too. I haven't seen you miss a throw since . . . shit, since I can't remember when."

Bridge sighed and began coiling his rope, twisting it to keep the loops roughly the same size. When he reached the honda, he adjusted the spoke and then swung the lasso overhead. "I asked him to move in. Sort of."

"No shit." Kent's horse snorted, as if the gelding were as piqued as Kent. "What do you mean 'sort of,' and what did he say?"

Bridge threw the coils and missed again. Barely ten fucking feet away. He sighed. "'Sort of' because I asked him to share our trailer on the road and then after the season, if he wanted to, move in here. Said he'd think about it, and then he up and took off right after breakfast. He called later and left a message to say he'd just meet us in Oakdale."

Kent was silent for a moment, and then said, "To be fair, that was kind of fast."

Bridge turned to glare at him. "We've known him the better part of a year now."

"Slow down, dude." Kent held up a hand. "Always gotta dive right in, don't you? Up 'til a couple of weeks ago, Eric thought you were straight. We all did. For the most part. So while you may have been thinking this through for months, he's only had weeks. Let him catch up. He'll get there. I've seen the way that man looks at you."

"Yeah?"

"Yeah. Dude's in deep. We have a ton of shit to get done ourselves before we roll out, so try not to worry. Okay?"

Bridge smiled for the first time since he'd waved good-bye to Eric, and that lightness when he'd realized how he felt about Eric seeped back in and soothed his worries. "You're right."

"Usually am," Kent said matter-of-factly and climbed down out of the saddle.

Bridge laughed and shook his head. "Lily like that cocky attitude of yours?"

"Oh no, I'm a smart dog. Lily's always right first."

# CHAPTER
## TWELVE

The first rodeo of the season in Oakdale, California, came and went, and Eric never showed up to work. Instead, some guy who looked barely out of high school but somehow managed to become a first responder saw to any injuries over the course of the weekend. The kid was competent enough, so Bridge couldn't begrudge him that, but he wasn't Eric and therefore, by default, was on Bridge's shit list.

What was even worse was that when he'd asked the kid where Eric was, all he'd gotten was a shoulder shrug and a nonchalant, "Quit, I think."

*Quit?*

Bridge had stood there a good five minutes until the words and situation truly sank in. Had he scared Eric so badly by asking him to pseudo move in that Eric felt he couldn't work the circuit with him anymore? Had Bridge moved so fast that he'd just gotten dumped with a no-show? A cold ball had formed in his chest, heavy and restricting, and he'd had to gulp for air. When he was finally able to catch his breath, he'd called Eric's cell again, but it went straight to voice mail—again. "You'd better not be doing what I think you're doing," was all he'd said in the first message. He'd been too upset at the time for levity. Fortunately, Marty had been able to get him focused on work, but it took everything he had in the long hours between start and end of the action to not go charging off to find Eric and shake some sense into the man.

Until today.

"I gotta go," Bridge said the second he and Marty rode out of the arena after the last official event of the rodeo three days later. He didn't even wait for an answer, just kicked his horse into a short gallop back to their rigs. When he slid to a stop and dismounted, Marty was right there.

"Here." Marty held out a hand, motioning for the reins. "I'll take care of Breeze. You go find Eric."

"Thank you, Smarts." Bridge handed Breeze's reins over. "I owe you."

"No, you don't." Marty dismounted and began leading the two horses to his trailer. "Get gone!"

And Bridge did. He unhitched the truck in record time and took off, driving as fast as was safe, which it really wasn't when the needle bumped up against the 100-mph line on the freeway. The longer he drove and the closer he got to Redding, the more he felt like time was running out. That if he didn't hurry up and get there already, he'd never see Eric again. He white-knuckled the steering wheel and fought to keep from pressing his foot down harder on the gas pedal.

Finally, he reached the CA-44 West exit and pulled off the I-5 into Redding. The sense of urgency that had been riding shotgun with him for the last three hours climbed into his seat and settled heavy on his chest. He had no idea why, but he knew time was almost up. It seemed like he'd turned onto one suburban street after another until he rounded yet another corner in a doglegged road and breathed a sigh of relief. There, in the driveway of a small, nondescript rancher, sat Eric's blue Tundra.

"Thank you, God," he whispered. But what he saw when he pulled up to the curb in front of the house made the blood in his veins turn to ice and his stomach plummet to his toes.

The door of the truck camper was open, and inside were boxes. A lot of boxes. The cab doors were open, and two boxes sat on the ground of the passenger side. And pitched at an angle in the small front yard . . . a For Sale sign.

Bridge climbed down from his truck and had to hold on to the side mirror for a second because the ground under his feet felt like it was shifting. His heart pounded hard in his chest, and his legs shook as he crossed the front lawn. Eric stepped out of the house with another box in his hands, and Bridge stopped dead in his tracks. Eric met his gaze and stumbled to a stop, the color draining from his face and shock filling his wide eyes.

"The hell?" Bridge said by way of hello.

Eric just stood there staring at him like a deer caught in headlights, the box in his arms beginning to cave with the force of his grip as he hugged it to his chest. "Bridge."

Bridge waited, not in the least bit patiently. Whatever Eric thought he was doing, he needed to step up and explain himself. Right fucking now. Because a week ago, they were in bed together, they were dating. A week ago, Eric had been inside of him. A week ago, he knew he was in love with a man who now seemed dead set on booking out of town without so much as an explanation.

A horn honked nearby, and Eric jumped, startling into action. "Ah. Why are you here?" He glanced away and then walked to the back of the truck, where he shoved the box inside then closed the door and locked it.

"Why am I here?" The edges of Bridge's vision turned crimson. Hurt and anger dueled with each other, and both tore at his heart. "Are you fucking serious?"

"I'm sorry. I meant to call earlier, but I've just been a bit busy." Eric dodged around the passenger side of the truck and picked up one of the boxes there, carelessly chucking it behind the seat like he was in a hurry. Pressure squeezed Bridge's chest, making it harder to breathe, while a cold chill seeped into his bones.

"With what? Moving away and not telling me?"

Eric shot a quick glance at him, like he was afraid to hold eye contact. "I, uh. I got a job offer out of state. One of those too-good-to-pass-up deals, and well . . . we both know this thing between us isn't going to work."

"Isn't going to work?" Bridge racked his brain, trying to figure out just what he'd done wrong, what signs he'd missed that he'd pushed Eric too far too fast. "No. We don't both know that. I thought it was working. I thought we were on the same page. And if this is about staying in my RV, or even moving in at the end of the season, I'm sorry. You know me—all guns blazing. I didn't mean to rush you. We can wait and see how things go, when you're ready. Just . . . don't leave."

"It's not that." Eric leaned down to pick up the next box and still seemed set on not making eye contact. His movements were jerky, and his accent was the thickest Bridge had ever heard it.

"Then what?" Bridge pleaded. "Tell me, and we'll work it out."

Eric slammed the door shut and walked back to the house, disappearing inside and leaving Bridge feeling oddly bereft. Like losing sight of the man had meant he'd lost him for real. But Eric hadn't closed the door behind him, so Bridge took that for the invitation he wanted it to be and followed.

He found Eric in a small bedroom, tossing items into a suitcase. His back was to Bridge, shoulders slumped, head down, and all Bridge wanted to do was wrap his arms around the man, tell him whatever the issue was they'd fix it. Together. He'd try to slow down and go at Eric's pace if only he wouldn't leave.

Eric sighed and straightened his shoulders, almost as if he were shoring up his resolve. He turned to face Bridge but didn't hold his gaze for more than a few seconds before turning back to his hasty packing. "You make me want things I can't have."

*What?* "That doesn't make any sense."

"Yes, it does. What you're offering me? It won't last. It might seem like it now, when things are all fresh and new, but before too long, you'll realize I'm really not what you want, and I'll be out on the streets again."

Bridge took a step forward, quiet on his feet as if he were approaching a frightened horse. He only had one chance to calm Eric and win his trust before he'd be lost forever to the wilds. "Again with the not making sense."

"I already told you!" Eric ran a hand over his head and spun around. He didn't look at Bridge though. He eyed the doorway instead, like he was gauging the distance between it and Bridge and whether or not he could make it out before Bridge could head him off. Jesus, what the hell had him spooked so badly?

He finally looked at Bridge then, straight in the eyes, and took a shaky breath. "Every single person who ever said they loved me threw me out. My own parents who should have loved me unconditionally dumped me in a foster home the second they found out I was gay. I was thirteen. No one adopts kids that old, and every single one of my foster families tossed me out. The few boyfriends I'd had promised me the world but dumped me as soon as a better piece of ass came along. And the guy I thought could have been the one was already fucking married to someone else. A woman. He said he loved me but not enough to leave his wife. Nobody wanted me for long. Ever."

"I do." Bridge tried to think of what he could say or do to make Eric understand, but the man was in a state, didn't seem to be able to hear. Keeping his voice smooth but firm and as articulate as he could manage, he said, "*I* want you."

"No." Eric shook his head in quick short twitches. "You think that now, and I might even let myself believe you. But you'll change your mind too. Like everyone else did. It's been fun, but before too long you'll realize I'm really not what you want, or that you prefer women after all. I mean, they can give you the family I can't. They're not going to get you beat up walking down the street holding hands."

"What the fuck is wrong with your head? You think this has just 'been fun'? A little experiment I'm going to tire of? How many times do I have to tell you I'm serious here? That *you* are the one I want?" He chanced another step forward, had to make Eric understand. "I don't want anyone but you, Eric. I *love you*."

Eric gasped, and Bridge's eyebrows shot up. He didn't regret saying it, not for a heartbeat. He meant it, he felt it, but he'd envisioned a nicer scenario when he finally said it. But instead of the declaration inciting joy, or at the very least easing some of Eric's fears, all the color drained from his face, his eyes widened, wild and unfocused, and his breath echoed in the small bedroom, shallow, hard, and fast.

"You need to leave." Eric's voice shook, but that didn't negate the force with which he spoke.

Bridge's heart clenched so tightly he thought it might shatter right then and there. The freezing cold continued to spread throughout his chest, up his throat, threatening to choke off the oxygen to his brain.

"Eric." It felt like shards of glass had been dragged up his throat as he pushed out the word, the splinters of his heart forcing their way out too. "I love you. With everything I have, everything I am. I want you in my life, and if you want a family, we can have one. There are plenty of ways to make that happen. Please, don't leave me."

Eric shook his head. "Nothing good ever lasts. That's the one true thing I've learned in this life. So let's leave it where it is. Okay? Let's leave what memories we have untainted by the bad that will come so they'll always be golden."

"Your past is not your future, Eric. I am not all those other people." He didn't know what he could say or do to reach Eric. It was like he was grasping at straws, drowning and the lifejacket was a finger-length beyond his reach, but he had to try. The alternative was unimaginable. "We can make this work. I know we can, if you just give us a chance. Deep down, I know you want this too."

"Fuck!" Eric shouted. Now he had Eric's full attention on him, but the violet fire in those eyes, the rage and hurt and fear were the last things Bridge wanted to see. "Do you know how many times I've been down this fucking road only to have it career off a cliff? I can't do it again. I will never survive you, Bridge. Oh, and the one time I thought I finally had a home for real, that I really was wanted, guess what happened? Guess! My foster mom had a fucking stroke and died! No." Eric shook his head vehemently. His nostrils flared, and his breath sounded so spent, he may as well have just run a marathon. He turned back to the case on the bed. "Nothing lasts, so it's best to get out while the getting's good. Before anyone gets hurt."

Bridge watched, stunned and speechless, as Eric closed up the last of his belongings in the suitcase. *You're hurting me right now*, he wanted to say, but his vocal chords had frozen shut. Eric chanced a quick glance at him and then shouldered past him, out of the room, out of the house. Eric was halfway down the driveway before Bridge shook out of his shocked state and ran after him.

"So that's it?" He reached for Eric, but the man maneuvered deftly out of his range. "If you keep running, you'll never escape your past."

"I'm not running. I have a new job." Eric's voice was flat, cold, emotionless. "Find someone else, Bridge. Someone who isn't afraid to be what you need."

"Don't do this, Eric. Please," Bridge pleaded, beyond caring if he got down on the ground and begged. Whatever it took to stop Eric from leaving. "You're the one. The only one for me."

Eric climbed up into the cab of his truck and slammed the door. The window was open. He fired up the truck and met Bridge's gaze. His eyes were flat and hard and devoid of emotion. "I'll never be anyone's one." Then he shifted the vehicle into gear and backed up, forcing Bridge to jump out of the way and let him go.

Bridge stood there in the empty driveway, dumbfounded, stricken, watching the only person he couldn't live without leave without a backward glance. "But you're my one and only."

The shattered pieces of his heart ripped and tore from his body, crashing to the ground at his feet in thunderous cracks, until all that was left in his chest was a massive, hollow hole. His entire body began to shake uncontrollably, gripped in a chill he already knew would never thaw.

Eric had just left him.

Eric. Left. Him.

He almost laughed at the irony of it all. Everyone had thought he'd be the one to break Eric's heart, but instead, Eric had not only broken Bridge's heart, he'd crushed it beyond repair and left it dying on crumbling, weed-lined concrete under a hot California sun.

# CHAPTER THIRTEEN

"**E**ric!"

He'd just stepped out of the Steamed Beans Café, next door to the Laundromat he'd been living above for the past five weeks, since his arrival in the small ski village of Steamboat Springs.

He turned to see Maggie Hewitt hustling toward him, her auburn hair dancing in the light breeze and a wide smile lighting her youthful face.

"I just wanted to say thank you," she said when she reached him, slightly out of breath. "That was so kind of you to come by the center. My mother can't stop talking about the handsome young man who brought her flowers, making all the other ladies jealous."

He'd tended to Maggie's mother when she'd taken a fall walking back from the grocery store the week before. She'd been so gracious and kind to him, when she was the one hurting, that he'd felt the need to stop by and check on her. He had noticed some of the other ladies at the center in a bit of a titter when he'd been there, and he smiled, remembering how bright Mrs. Hewitt's eyes had glittered at the stir. "How is she doing?"

"Much better, thanks to you." Maggie reached up and placed her hand gently on his cheek. "You're a wonderful person, Eric. I hope you have someone to give you as much joy as you give others."

His heart clenched, his throat constricted, and tears pricked at his eyes. One second he was fine and the next he was on the verge of breaking down and crying like a baby right there on Main Street in broad daylight. He did have someone, but he'd been too much of a coward to see that.

"Thank you, Maggie," he managed. He gave her hand a light squeeze. "I've, uh . . . I've gotta go." Without waiting for a response, he turned and practically sprinted the few feet to his building's door.

He ran up the stairs two at a time and slammed his door behind him. His eyes tracked the room he'd rented when he'd pulled into town after making the biggest mistake of his life. There was a kitchenette, a bathroom big enough for a narrow shower stall, and a living room-slash-bedroom featuring an old pull-out couch, a secondhand coffee table, two end tables, and one lamp. The room looked as transient as he felt there, even though he had a good job, and now knew every local by name and they, him.

Maggie's mother wasn't the first person he'd ever followed up with after an accident, wasn't the first person who thought he was so wonderful and deserving. But they didn't know him, and that was part of his job. It made him feel good to have a positive impact on people's lives in small ways, so why couldn't he accept the same in return? Why hadn't he been able to accept that Bridge truly had wanted to give him joy, had loved him?

Because through work or helping strangers there was a sense of safety in that detachment, but when that barrier was crossed and his heart came into play . . . Everyone had hurt him. How could he believe Bridge would be any different?

*Because he is, and you know it.*

Eric pressed a hand to his chest at the thought of the handsome cowboy, as if it could ease the pain that had yet to lessen. He sat down on the couch and tossed his phone onto the table, staring at it as if that would make it ring. If it rang now, he'd answer, but of course it didn't. He'd made sure that wouldn't happen either.

He reached out and picked up the phone, sliding his thumb over the surface. Bridge was in there. He'd called every day that first week, but Eric hadn't answered. Too ashamed of how he'd run, too afraid to hear pain or anger in Bridge's voice, and with no idea what to say to fix it. He'd listened to every message, and the broken, defeated tone in Bridge's voice haunted his every waking and sleeping minute.

If he called now, would Bridge talk to him? Could Bridge really need, or even want, him back?

Not if he were judged on how he'd left Bridge—broken and alone in the driveway of his house in Redding. He'd known in that moment that he'd made a huge mistake. But he hadn't been able to turn around, too caught up in the past to take the future into his hands . . . to put it in Bridge's and just trust him.

Too much of a coward to put his heart on the line, he'd broken Bridge's instead.

He knew the second it happened because he'd felt the pain as his own, and maybe that had scared him even more, because in that moment, he'd realized that somewhere along the way, he'd fallen in love with Bridge too.

*Shit.* He stood up, dropped the phone on the table with a loud *clank*, and started pacing the small room. All that time he'd tried to keep himself from falling too deep into the rabbit hole, and he'd managed to fall into another one. He couldn't pinpoint the moment when he did, but he knew now, without a doubt, that he was in love with Bridge.

And he'd run from the one person who'd given him every reason to stay.

For the next two days, Eric was barely able to concentrate on his work. Everything in him screamed at him to pack up and go back to California, back to Bridge, but the what-ifs kept him numb and static. What if Bridge wouldn't take him back? What if Bridge didn't love him anymore? Or never really had? What if Bridge had moved on already and had a girlfriend?

What if Eric just grew a pair and fought for the cowboy who'd only wanted to give him everything?

He sighed and pushed open the front door to the Steamed Beans Café, scanning the dining room for Carl, the owner. Carl stood behind the bakery display case making a coffee, and when he looked up, he paused for a second before a small smile lifted the edges of his mouth. He tipped his head, and Eric followed the motion to an empty table by the window.

Carl was one-part town busybody, one-part shrink, one-part psychic, and wholly genuine. The locals felt comfortable talking to him because he always seemed to know the right thing to say at the right time. He was one of those people with an uncanny knack for putting those around him at ease. Eric included. But Eric hadn't yet shared his story, and Carl never pressed for it.

He regarded the old man who lowered himself into the seat across from him, wise gray eyes studying, searching, as he slid a cup of coffee in front of Eric.

"Heard you went back to the hospital to make sure that boy you pulled from the Yampa was okay," Carl said. "Heard what you did for Maggie's ma, too."

Eric shrugged. "Just doing my job."

"Your job ended as soon as you delivered them to the ER."

Eric looked out the small café window at the mountains that rose up and surrounded Steamboat Springs. He wanted to tell Carl his story, but now that he was here, he didn't know where to start. Or how.

Carl, being the intuitive man that he was, thankfully got the ball rolling for him. "Awful dark cloud hanging over you lately, son."

Eric pushed out a pent-up breath and ran a hand through his hair. He hadn't had it cut since he'd left California, and now it was just long enough to run his fingers through. "I screwed up, Carl. Bad."

"We all screw up sometime. That's life. It's how we deal with it that matters."

"I haven't been dealing with it very well at all." He looked down into the black liquid in his cup, as if the future might reveal itself there.

"Never too late to start."

"My life hasn't been . . . great. There's been some good for sure. I love my work and love being able to help people. Maybe make a few smile. But . . ." Eric shrugged and took a sip of his coffee. "Let's just say I haven't had a lot of reason to believe good things can happen to me too."

Carl nodded for him to go on, those wise gray eyes patient and compassionate.

"I met someone who made me think maybe this time would be different, and I got scared because this one . . ." He rolled his shoulders back and looked right into Carl's eyes. "I love him, and I'm scared to death history will keep repeating itself and he'll leave me like everyone else. I couldn't bear it if he did that, so I fucked it all up and left him first."

Carl didn't even blink at the confession. "Can't do nothing about the past, but you can control what you do in the present. That's what makes your future."

"Bridge said something like that once." Eric huffed a halfhearted laugh.

"So why are you still here?" There was no malice or menace in the older man's voice, just open sincerity.

Eric cupped the mug in his hands and frowned at the dregs in the bottom, having not remembered drinking the whole cup. "I doubt he'll take me back now. I hurt him, and it's been weeks."

"Won't know unless you try, will you? Pack up your truck and get on back home." Carl stood and gathered the empty coffee cup. He came around the table and gave Eric's shoulder a squeeze. His gruff voice benevolent, he said, "That's where you belong, son."

Carl had disappeared into the kitchen by the time Eric got up to leave. He stepped out onto the sidewalk, looked up and down the street, and then turned his face to the sky, closing his eyes. Warm spring sunshine kissed his cheeks, and instead of his heart weeping for the one he'd left behind, it sang for the hope that they'd be together again.

Time to stop being a coward, let all the what-ifs go, and take his future by the horns.

He walked around the corner and down to the river, where he found a vacant bench to sit on.

Inhaling a calming breath, he tapped the screen and pulled up his contacts, selected a number, and before he could second-guess himself, hit the Send key, and raised the phone to his ear.

Today was the day he'd start putting the past behind him.

His pulse picked up when a familiar voice answered, and the ache in his chest eased a little. Fuck, he'd missed them all so much, but he hadn't realized how much until right now. Carl was right; he belonged back in California. He belonged with Bridge, if the cowboy would take him back.

"Hello, Marty."

"Thank God!" The relief in Marty's voice gave Eric pause. He'd expected fury, a ranting knock down. But relief? "I'm so glad you called. We were worried about you." Marty paused. "But, fuck man. You seriously pissed us all off."

There was the response Eric had expected. "I know. I'm so sorry. I just . . ."

"Yeah. Bridge told us what happened. But you didn't have to run from all of us. You know that, right?"

"At the time I didn't."

Silence crackled down the line long enough for him to think Marty had hung up. His throat tightened, and he fought back the rush of tears building behind his eyes, closing his lids to contain them. "How's Bridge?" His voice was ragged, the words choked off, and he dreaded the answer, but he had to know.

That heavy silence continued, and then a sigh rattled in his ear. "Not well. You took part of what made him who he was with you when you left. And, well . . . I'm kind of selfish and I want it back."

A single sob managed to slip through Eric's control, and the tears found their way out, making a run for freedom down his cheeks. "I never wanted to hurt him."

"I know." Marty's voice was soft, more caring than he deserved. "Where are you?"

"Uh . . ." Eric swiped a sleeve across his face. "Colorado. Steamboat Springs."

"We'll be in Santa Maria this weekend." Marty didn't have to say more, the intention in his words was clear.

Santa Maria. The rodeo where Eric had first met the three cowboys who'd become the best friends he'd ever known. Where he'd first met Bridge Sullivan—the man who owned his heart hook, line, and sinker.

"Come back, Eric." Marty's voice was gentle, comforting, sincere. "We miss you. Bridge misses you. You belong here with him."

*Yes, I do.*

No fear lodged in his chest at that thought, no flight instinct overruling all rational thought—just a sense of complete rightness. "If he'll take me back."

"He will. He won't kick you to the curb, and neither will we. You're part of our family, Eric, and family doesn't turn on itself."

"Some do," Eric said.

Marty responded with conviction. "Not this one. Not ever. We all make mistakes, Eric. It's how we deal with them, right?"

*And prove our worth.* "Right."

"Good. Glad that's settled. Now get in your little Tonka truck and get your ass back here."

The band that had been strung tight across Eric's chest eased for the first time in weeks, and the laugh that rumbled up his throat was the first genuine one since he'd left California. "Will do."

When Bridge rounded the faux-half-circle created by his and Marty's trailers, he found the guys in a group hug with someone. He didn't know who and really didn't care. He was in no mood for making nice with anyone. The first half of day one at the Santa Maria rodeo hadn't been going well. Already they'd had three accidents, one of which sent a barrel racer to the hospital with a concussion and possible internal injuries.

He ignored the happy trio, reined Breeze to the side of the trailer, and dismounted, keeping his back to the world.

"Bridge!" Kent called out, excitement clear in his voice. "Look who's here."

With a groan and an eye roll, because he really didn't give a shit, Bridge turned around and promptly froze.

Eric, live and in the flesh, stood between Marty and Kent like he'd never been gone a day. Looking better than anybody had the right to, wearing worn jeans, a button-down shirt with the sleeves pushed up to reveal muscular forearms . . . and snakeskin boots and a brown felt cowboy hat.

For a brief second, joy bubbled up in his chest. Someone turned the sun back on, and warmth started to push out the chill that seemed to have sunk permanently into his bones.

"Hey," Eric said, his voice and small smile both tentative. Eyes uncertain.

And that brief second of warmth popped like a balloon.

*Hey?* Six weeks of nothing. No calls, no messages, no *nothing*, then he has the gall to show up and say *Hey*? Like he'd just been off on a happy little jaunt with Bridge's blessing and now that he was back everything would be peachy keen again?

No.

The dead place in his mind widened to replay the scene all those weeks ago. The scene where he'd stood motionless and numb all alone in an empty driveway until the sun had gone down and the desert night air had grown colder than the freeze of his heart. He'd somehow managed to get himself back to the rodeo grounds and continue on with the motions of daily life. Had continued to breathe air in and breathe air out without really knowing why anymore. And now that familiar cold began to spread in his bones again, freezing out the brief promise of relief.

Without responding, Bridge turned back to his horse and began unbuckling the cinch strap. He had things to do. Cool down and groom Breeze, get Gameboy saddled up and ready for the afternoon events. Stay on his game and do his job. Not think about Eric Palmer standing right behind him with those haunting violet eyes burning holes in his back just like they'd been burning holes in his dreams every night for the last month and a half.

Throats cleared. Boots shuffled. The sound of a hand clapping a back drifted the dozen feet or so to his ears. Kent's voice low. "Good to see you, Eric. I hope you're sticking around." One set of footsteps faded away. Then Marty's voice, too quiet to make out the words he spoke, but his tone was friendly, supportive.

His so-called brothers were fucking traitors.

Another single set of footsteps faded away. He knew it was just him and Eric then, and he'd be damned if he'd turn around.

Bootheels sounded quietly on the hard dirt, and then Eric's resonant voice danced near his ear, closer than he'd thought. "Bridge, can we talk?"

"Talk?" Bridge snorted and shot a glare over his shoulder. "Made it pretty clear you didn't want to talk for the last six weeks. Can't imagine why you'd want to now."

"I made a mistake."

"Don't we all." Cinch and flank straps undone, Bridge slid the saddle off Breeze's back, leaned it pommel-down against the trailer, and turned the saddle blanket sweat-side up on the ground to dry out.

"Bridge. I'm so sorry." The raw pain in Eric's voice, too familiar to the agony Bridge had been living with, dug into him and pulled at wounds that wouldn't close. "The last thing I ever wanted to do was hurt you, but I was so scared."

The steady ache Bridge had come to live with spiked, pinched tight in his chest like it had that fateful day in April, and he turned to face Eric. Up close, he didn't look much better than Bridge felt. His cheeks were sunken, he'd lost weight, his skin was an ashen color, and his normally vibrant violet eyes were dull. "Scared of what? Me?" Fuck, that hurt.

"No!" Eric said quickly, and then he looked down and Bridge saw more than heard the deep breath Eric swallowed. "Yes. Scared of you loving me. Scared of loving you back. Scared of you leaving me because everyone who ever said they loved me left me. How could I ever believe it could be true after it being a lie my whole life? But I was wrong. So very wrong, and I see that now, and I'm trying not to be scared anymore. Because a wise cowboy once told me that my past isn't my future, and I'm trying to be stronger for him." Eric took off the hat Bridge had given him the day after his birthday, right before he'd bolted, and ran a hand over hair that was much longer than it had been the last time Bridge had seen him.

"Can we . . . Do you think?" He looked up to meet Bridge's gaze head-on. "Do you think there's a chance for us? That we can try again?"

God, he wanted to, but he didn't think he could. Not yet. "You broke my heart, Eric."

"I know. I'm so sorry." Eric fidgeted with the brim of the hat in his hands. "If I could go back and change things, I would."

"I don't know that I can ever risk that again."

"I understand. I do." Eric's eyes began to shine, and Bridge couldn't hold his gaze any longer. The always-present ache in his chest increased, squeezed tight around his heart. He didn't think he could hurt any more than he had been, but seeing how much Eric hurt too, feeling waves of remorse and anguish radiate from the man made Bridge want to throw all his caution to the wind and pull him into his arms, hold him close, tell him everything would work out, that they'd see to it. But he couldn't. The pain of his own heartbreak was still too fresh and raw.

Bridge cleared his throat and looked away, grabbing a halter from the tack box that sat on the trailer tire well. "I gotta get to work."

Eric jumped back. "Sure. Yeah."

Bridge exchanged Breeze's bridle for the halter and turned to walk her until she cooled down.

"Bridge." He stopped at the sound of Eric's voice tight with an undertone of panic. "I'm staying at the Super 8 just down the highway. I'll be there through the weekend, 'til Monday. If—" His voice hitched. "—if you change your mind."

Bridge didn't turn around, didn't nod, didn't do anything to let Eric know he'd heard him. Then he took a deep breath and, with eyes forward, moved on.

# CHAPTER
## FOURTEEN

E ric looked at his watch for the seventeenth time in as many minutes, and then glared at the door again for good measure. He willed a knock to sound from the other side, but it remained as frustratingly silent as it had all weekend.

The Santa Maria rodeo had officially ended yesterday afternoon. Motel check-out time was officially seventeen minutes ago. The knock he longed for was never coming.

Not a surprise really. He had no one to blame but himself.

He'd been so afraid of the past repeating itself that he'd been the one to ensure it did. He could see that clearly now.

He'd turned away the one man who'd become everything to him, who'd deserved the trust he'd asked for. Who he'd fallen in love with when he'd been fighting to keep himself from getting in too deep.

He glanced at his watch again. As if eighteen would be the magic number of minutes that would bring that coveted knock. If the knock came, it would probably only be the motel staff coming to kick him out so they could clean the room—or charge him for another night. But Bridge wasn't coming. Eric had seen to that.

With a heavy heart and heavier body, he stood and grabbed his duffel bag, crossed the small motel room he'd been pacing in for the last two days, and opened the door. He peered out, scanning the walkway and parking lot beyond, half-hoping Bridge would be there, standing outside the door waiting, or be in the parking lot leaning against his massive Dodge Ram, with his hat tipped down and a sultry grin on his handsome face.

But there was nothing.

The walkway, the parking lot, and the street in both directions as far as he could see from his motel room door were empty and deserted. Like the rock in his chest that would have to pass for a heart from this point on. Like he'd always figured was his lot in life.

Only it wasn't.

If he'd just gotten out of his own way.

If he'd just trusted in Bridge, trusted in them.

If he hadn't manifested his own worst fears into reality.

And in the end he'd lost everything. More than Bridge. He'd lost brotherhood and family and love. A place where, for a time, he'd belonged.

But that final tendril of hope was lost forever, and his whole body caved in on itself. He sucked in a painful breath of air, adjusted the cowboy hat on his head—that and the boots were the only things he still had to tie him to Bridge—and walked to his truck, the echo of his heavy, lonely footfalls following him. He climbed into the cab and stuck the key in the ignition but didn't turn the engine over. He was stalling. He knew it was pointless, but couldn't help himself.

The final nail in his coffin would be having no choice but to drive past the empty rodeo grounds on his way back to Colorado. The longer he didn't leave, the longer he could put off the indisputable evidence that Bridge was gone from his life forever.

"Fuck!"

He smacked the steering wheel with the heel of his hand and cranked the ignition. The truck responded with an angry snarl and jumped forward when he slammed it into gear and accelerated too fast out of the parking lot and onto the deserted street.

The closer he got to the rodeo grounds, the tighter he gripped the wheel, the harder he pressed his lips together, and the faster his pulse pounded. Some little holdout of hope started peeking its head out of the darkness only to be hacked away by a dull, rusted blade.

The grounds were empty.

He yanked his eyes away and stared hard at the stretch of pavement ahead as his vision blurred, threatening to force him to the side of the road. He swiped away the tears with his sleeve and forced the rest back. He would not let them fall. He'd carry them with him for the rest of his life. Penance. A permanent reminder of what his fears had cost him.

Another half hour down the highway, blessedly numb, he noticed an approaching truck. It was black. Bridge's Dodge was black. The vehicle grew larger on the horizon and Eric was able to discern the make as a Dodge Ram 3500—a big-ass truck like Bridge's. Heading the opposite direction for Hesperia, which was the next stop on the circuit.

Eric rolled his hands on the steering wheel. Fuck. Every time he saw a big black Dodge from now on, he was going to immediately hope, for just a second, that it would be Bridge.

Closer now, he could make out the shape of the driver—a big man like Bridge wearing a black cowboy hat . . . like Bridge.

One hundred feet. Hope began to rise. Fifty feet. His pulse quickened. Twenty-five feet. His heart launched into his throat.

It *was* Bridge.

They passed each other on a highway traveling at sixty miles per hour, yet time somehow slowed down. Stuttered until the frame froze. His gaze locked on Bridge's, the split-second stare spanning out for what felt like an hour, but Eric couldn't get a read on Bridge's expression.

And like releasing a stretched elastic band, time snapped back to regular speed and the big Dodge was in his rearview mirror, getting smaller by the second. Red taillights remained dark, and the truck continued to shrink in his mirror.

"No!" His voice rang in his own ears. "You came back! You can't change your mind now!"

Eric slammed on the brakes and cranked the wheel hard. The vehicle teetered on its axles while deciding whether to grant the sudden U-turn or give up the rubber and flip over. Bridge had come back for him. That was all that mattered. Even if his truck rolled and he had to run on his own two feet to catch that man, he would. No way, no how was anything going to stop him now. His future was his own to create.

With a final heart-pounding skid, he straightened the vehicle and floored it, just in time to see two red eyes flash before they blinked out and became two bright-white lights. Bridge had turned around. Bridge was coming for him.

At a hundred feet away, Eric pulled off the road and slid to a sideways stop on the shoulder, tires kicking up a tornado of dust. Bridge copied his move and came to a dust-swirling stop on the opposite shoulder, almost directly across the highway.

Eric couldn't get the door open quickly enough, but adrenaline pumped too fast through his veins and the frantic need to get out *right now* messed with his coordination. Finally, the handle released, and he spilled out of the cab. He hit the ground running, not stopping until he slammed into Bridge in the middle of the deserted road.

And there, straddling the centerline on a two-lane highway, locked in a bone-crushing hug, Eric's life began. The tears came hot and heavy, flushing away his every fear, his every doubt, his every pain, and clearing the way for a new journey.

"I'm so sorry." He sobbed into Bridge's shoulder. "I was such an idiot."

"Yes, you were, but that's behind us now. Right?" Bridge's voice sounded tight, like maybe he was on the verge of crying too.

"Right." Eric nodded, swallowing hard through a constricted throat. "I didn't think you were going to come."

Bridge pulled back but didn't let go. Eric wouldn't have let him anyway. "My first reaction when I saw you the other day was joy. I hadn't felt anything but cold and empty since you left, so that had to mean something. One look and you gave me back the sunshine. You hurt me more than anything, but underneath that, I still love you. I've never loved anyone like I love you, Eric Palmer. How could I let you go a second time?"

"Bridge, I—" Before he could finish, Bridge swooped in and claimed his mouth in a desperate, all-consuming kiss that he submitted to instantly and completely. Anything Bridge wanted. He would spend the rest of his life doing everything in his power to make Bridge happy. To be the man Bridge deserved. The need for oxygen forced him to break the kiss when his head started feeling dizzy. That or he was just so overwhelmingly happy to be back in Bridge's arms. Where he belonged.

"Plus, we had to work right up until they closed the grounds, so we had to book it out of there. I left Kent with the horses at the first rest area we came upon, and then hightailed it back," Bridge said. "I'd have driven all the way to Colorado to catch you."

He looked up into those rich chocolate-colored eyes and took the first easy breath since he'd foolishly left Bridge. He didn't care. All that mattered was that Bridge was here, had come back for him. "I love you, cowboy."

Bridge tapped the brim of Eric's hat and grinned. The playful one that never failed to cast a ray of sunshine in his mind. "Took you long enough to figure it out."

Eric smiled. "Guess I had to learn how to let it ride."

# EPILOGUE

"**D**on't be sad, Uncle Eric."

Eric looked down to find wide, blue eyes staring up at him. His vision blurred, but he blinked quickly until it cleared. "I'm not sad, honey."

Karlee, Barrett's youngest daughter, stepped closer and slipped her tiny hand over his, giving comfort, and his heart squeezed at the gesture. She leaned in and whispered, "But you're crying."

Eric wiped a thumb across his cheek, and it came away wet. He'd been so lost in his thoughts, he hadn't realized he'd teared up. He smiled at Karlee. "I'm just really happy."

She frowned in that exaggerated-yet-adorable way kids did.

"Sometimes when people are really happy, the emotion gets too big to keep inside," he said. "One way to let it out is tears."

Her frown deepened. "That's silly."

"I suppose it is." He kissed her forehead. "But I'm really good. Promise."

She studied him for a moment, chewing on her bottom lip, expression dubious, and then nodded. "Okay."

He smiled, watching her skip out of the dining room back to whatever mischief the rest of Bridge's nieces and nephews were getting up to. He turned his attention back to the people sitting around the table, and that overwhelming sense of joy spread throughout his chest again. Just like he had at last year's birthday dinner for Bridge, Eric sat between the oldest and youngest Sullivan brothers, both laughing while Bill regaled them with a story whose punch line Eric had missed. Grandpa Abe made sure no one's wineglass ran dry, while Lenora made sure everyone had full plates. There was another new addition this year, though, with Marty's sister Lily joining the festivities after having finally been convinced that Kent was the man for her.

These were *his* friends, this was *his* family, and he couldn't remember ever having been this truly, deeply happy in all his life.

He reached out and rested his hand on Bridge's thigh, and without looking, Bridge slipped his hand under the table and laced their fingers together. He lifted their joined hands to his lips and kissed Eric's knuckles, and Eric's vision blurred again.

"Hey." Bridge looked at him, those warm, sincere eyes barely visible through long bangs that Eric loved to slide his fingers through so much. "Are you okay?"

He nodded. "Better than." And he was. He'd finally found that elusive place to belong, found the love he'd never believed himself worthy of. Found a true home with Bridge. With the cowboys who'd become his best friends. With the family who'd taken him in as one of their own from the very moment they'd met.

How he'd managed to get so lucky, he didn't know, but it was real.

Bridge leaned in and placed a quick kiss on his lips, then stood up, pulling Eric with him. "Mom, we're going to get some fresh air before dessert."

Lenora's face lit up, as if Bridge had just told her she'd won the lottery instead of that he was stepping outside. Someone cleared a throat, loudly, and a light flush filled her cheeks. Her gaze slid between him and Bridge, and then she casually said, "Of course, sweetheart. Take your time."

"But not too long," Marty said. Eric didn't miss the note of excitement in his voice or the expression on his face, either. "Celebrations await."

Bridge led them to a bench that overlooked a large fishpond in the back garden. The night was warm for early spring, and a low-hanging moon reflected in the dark pool, shimmering like diamonds.

When they stopped, Eric hooked a finger through one of Bridge's belt loops, tugging him closer. "What was that all about?"

"What was what?"

"Don't play coy with me, cowboy."

Bridge only smiled and then cupped his face in his large, rough hands. "I love you."

Every time Bridge said those words, *meant* those words, Eric felt as if his heart grew a little bigger, that the light in his mind shone a little brighter. He had finally gotten out of his own way, let the past go, and come to believe it, to trust in Bridge, in them. "I love you too."

Eric slid a hand behind Bridge's head and pulled him down. Their lips met in a slow, deep kiss. Bridge fisted one hand into the hair Eric had grown out a little, while the other traced down the side of his neck, over his collarbone to rest on his chest, and for just a second, Eric could imagine his heart literally in Bridge's hand. Eric angled his head to deepen the kiss, slipped his tongue into Bridge's mouth, and drew a deep moan from his eager cowboy. God, he loved how Bridge gave everything in himself every single time they touched.

The hand on his chest moved, made a crooked trail back up and over his shoulder, down his biceps, forearm, and to his hand. He attempted to twine their fingers, but Bridge evaded the move and held on to one finger. He broke the kiss, dropped his other hand from Eric's hair, and stepped back half a foot. Eric tried to chase Bridge's mouth, but something metallic shining near the end of the finger Bridge had captured drew his attention.

He glanced down, and his breath caught. His heart shot into high gear. He blinked. Moonlight glinted off a silver ring Bridge had pushed only as far as the nail bed of the third digit of his left hand. He looked up into eyes as dark as the night surrounding them, just as warm, comforting, safe . . . and full of love. Love for him.

"Say yes," Bridge whispered.

"Yes. Hell yes."

Bridge pushed the ring all the way onto his finger, and it was like the last piece of a puzzle finally slotted into place and fused there. He'd been happy with things as they were but hadn't realized until now, with this ring, that there'd been one little kernel of doubt still floating around.

He wrapped his arms around Bridge, pulled them as tightly together as possible, and kissed Bridge for all he was, for every dream Eric had been afraid to reach for, and all the hope he'd tried to bury. He kissed the man who'd taught him he was worthy of it all.

A loud whistle and whoop shocked the kiss to an abrupt end, and Eric jumped back. Behind him, the entire family, *his* entire family, and his friends stood at the edge of the garden. Every face was lit with happiness and wide smiles, clapping, whistling, and hollering their congratulations.

"You all knew?" He turned back to Bridge and glared, but he couldn't stop the smile from breaking out across his face.

Bridge laughed beside him, wrapping an arm around his shoulders, and pulled him tight to his side. He leaned down and whispered in Eric's ear. "Thank you."

"For what?"

"Letting me love you."

He turned in Bridge's arms, putting into the kiss all the words he couldn't speak just then.

On a warm spring evening under a moonlit sky, surrounded by friends and family, in the arms of the man he loved, he was finally home.

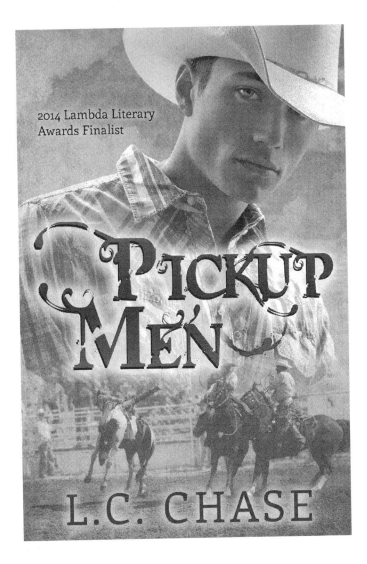

2014 Lambda Literary
Awards Finalist

PICKUP
MEN

L.C. CHASE

Dear Reader,

Thank you for reading L.C. Chase's *Let It Ride*!

We know your time is precious and you have many, many entertainment options, so it means a lot that you've chosen to spend your time reading. We really hope you enjoyed it.

We'd be honored if you'd consider posting a review—good or bad—on sites like **Amazon, Barnes & Noble, Kobo, Goodreads, Twitter, Facebook, Tumblr,** and your blog or website. We'd also be honored if you told your friends and family about this book. Word of mouth is a book's lifeblood!

For more information on upcoming releases, author interviews, blog tours, contests, giveaways, and more, please sign up for our weekly, spam-free newsletter and visit us around the web:

**Newsletter:** tinyurl.com/RiptideSignup
**Twitter:** twitter.com/RiptideBooks
**Facebook:** facebook.com/RiptidePublishing
**Goodreads:** tinyurl.com/RiptideOnGoodreads
**Tumblr:** riptidepublishing.tumblr.com

Thank you so much for Reading the Rainbow!

RiptidePublishing.com

# ALSO BY
# L.C. CHASE

Pickup Men (Pickup Men, #1)
Love Brokers: Mister Romance
Riding with Heaven
Long Tall Drink

# ABOUT THE AUTHOR

Cover artist by day, author by night, L.C. Chase is a hopeless romantic and adventure seeker. After a decade of traveling three continents, she now calls the Canadian West Coast home. When not writing sensual tales of beautiful men falling love, she can be found designing book covers with said beautiful men, drawing, horseback riding, or hiking the trails with her goofy four-legged roommate.

L.C. is a 2014 Lambda Literary Award Finalist for *Pickup Men*; a 2013 EPIC eBook Awards Finalist for *Long Tall Drink*; and a 2013-2014 Ariana eBook Cover Art Awards Finalist. She also won an honorable mention in the 2012 Rainbow Awards for *Riding with Heaven*.

You can visit L.C. at www.lcchase.com.

# Enjoyed this book?
Visit RiptidePublishing.com and discover more first-time bisexual romance!

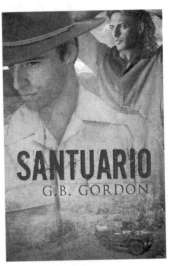

*Straight Shooter*
ISBN: 978-1-62649-090-1

*Santuario*
ISBN: 978-1-937551-65-0

## Earn Bonus Bucks!

Earn 1 Bonus Buck for each dollar you spend. Find out how at RiptidePublishing.com/news/bonus-bucks.

## Win Free Ebooks for a Year!

Pre-order coming soon titles directly through our site and you'll receive one entry into a drawing to win free books for a year! Get the details at RiptidePublishing.com/contests.

21991409R00104

Made in the USA
San Bernardino, CA
21 June 2015